AMISH MYSTERIES: HAUNTED

AN AMISH MYSTERY BOOK

RUTH PRICE

GLOBAL GRAFX PRESS

CONTENTS

ABOUT THIS BOOK

Everyone knew the old Crawley house was haunted. What if everyone was right?

They say the Crawley house is haunted, but Luke King knows better. When his brother comes home claiming the ghost attacked him, Luke vows to prove it all Noah's overactive imagination. What Luke finds will transform himself and his Amish district forever.

After discovering the truth of her best friend, Salome's disappearance, Susie Zook is haunted by her mistakes. If only she had spoken up, Salome might still be alive. But when Salome's killer returns, Susie vows to protect her home and family, even if she must commit a terrible crime.

With two women's lives in the balance, ghosts of the past collide with sins of the present in this suspenseful Amish mystery novel. Can Luke protect the woman he loves? Will Susie forgive her best friend's killer? Find out in Haunted, Book 2 of the Amish Mystery series.

PROLOGUE

*E*veryone knew the old Crawley house was haunted. Five winters back, Susie found Salome there in a shallow grave beneath an old oak strung with red ribbons. Salome's favorite. Beanpole had killed her. Manslaughter. English doctors said the cause was madness not malice.

Susie blamed silence, secrets, and herself.

English law sent Beanpole for psychiatric rehabilitation, which was a nice way of saying they locked him away in a nuthouse. Forgive and forget, emphasis on forget.

Except after five years, the doctors sent him home. People who *manslaughtered* people weren't supposed to come back. Maybe that's what had Salome riled up.

God knew. The four eleven-year-old boys, huddled on the other side of the fence, shaking in their English boots with more bravado than sense, didn't.

"You think it's really her ghost?" Noah asked, clutching at the fence post, breath curling out in a damp cloud. He was stick thin, shrouded in a heavy coat, long johns, trousers and an English-style ski hat, one of his three most treasured possessions.

Thomas, a heavy-boned boy with a round, chubby face, glasses with thick, dark frames, and a respect, or, more accurately, fear of authority instilled in him by four older sisters, asked, "If she was an innocent, wouldn't she go to heaven?"

Thomas, through no fault of his own, was a grubby, faded version of himself. Hair like an old penny, eyes the new green of spring grass, a smudge on his cheek and dirt beneath his half new moon fingernails, which no matter how often his sisters demanded he scrubbed, never quite came clean. He had lost his gloves again and stuffed his large fists into the pockets of his navy coat.

Samuel, who also wore glasses and went, not by choice, by Sammy, said, "A ghost will linger if it has unfinished business."

Sammy spoke with authority. His second oldest

brother, also named Samuel, had a library card and brought home English novels about murder, stalkers, spirits, and other horrors which Sammy stayed up late reading by the lantern after stuffing a blanket beneath the door so his parents didn't notice. Even without the reference, Sammy was a kid who knew things. And if he didn't, he made them up until he believed them. Lying was a sin, but not if you believed what you were saying.

Daniel, the fourth and least popular member of their band said, "That old house is full of rats."

"Rats only stay if there's something to eat." Sammy said with confidence.

"Beanpole left food for her," Daniel said.

Noah snorted. "Three years ago. The rats would have eaten it all up by now. Or maybe she did, if ghosts eat."

"Some ghosts can feast on your soul," Sammy said. "They suck it right out and walk around inside your skin until your body rots."

All four boys shivered.

Noah, the bravest because he had nothing else if he wasn't brave, said, "Ach! I dare her to do it! If Salome was going to suck out somebody's soul and devour it, she would've eaten Beanpole's. He's the one who killed her."

"Katie," Thomas said, referring to his second oldest sister, "said it was an accident. Beanpole didn't mean to kill her."

"Maybe," Sammy said adjusting his glasses—which were smaller than Thomas's—narrow ovals with wireframes. "Maybe Salome didn't want to wear Beanpole's body. Nobody much liked him, even before he killed her."

"Beanpole's different since he got back," Noah said, remembering the last church meeting. Beanpole had stared at the bishop, glassy-eyed, mouth opened, with a slick tear of drool glistening on his bottom lip. "Slow." Noah wouldn't have heard the end of it if he acted like that at Church meeting, but Noah hadn't killed anyone.

"That's the medication," Thomas said. "Hannah explained it." Hannah was Thomas's oldest sister, now married to Owen Schrock.

Daniel said, "Good. Since it's just the medication, why don't you go check and see if she's still there?"

Thomas asked, "What does one thing have to do with the other?"

"You're scared."

"Ghosts aren't real. I just don't see the point in trespassing." Thomas pulled his chapped hand from his pocket and patted the knuckle beneath his nose, which had begun to run. "Katie will have me washing dishes and carrying all the groceries for weeks if she finds out I was trespassing."

"You carry the groceries, anyway. I see you, in town."

"Not every week."

"I bet you're scared of the rats." Daniel taunted. "I bet they are all over. In the walls and floors, staring up through the holes."

"If you want to see the ghost, you go in there."

Daniel let rip a whistling fart. It was his best and most effective way of changing the subject.

"Ewwww!" the others sang in an off-beat choir.

Daniel giggled. Noah joined in. He wouldn't back down to flatulence.

Thomas wrinkled his nose. "You are so gross!"

"No ghost will come near me."

"Ghosts don't have a sense of smell," Sammy said. He angled away from Tom, as though looking at the house, and put a finger under his nostrils in a pose of thinking more intended to mitigate the stench. "But try it, if you want."

"You're all scaredy-cats," Daniel said. "Even Noah."

Noah glanced at the house. If there was a

ghost inside, he didn't want to meet it. But he couldn't back down. Not from Daniel, who was as scared on the inside as Thomas was cautious on the outside.

Noah said, "I'll go. I 'ent scared. If Salome's haunting anyone, it's Beanpole."

Sammy said, "Maybe we should make the spirit an offering."

"Like what?"

"Blood!" Daniel said. "Tom, do you have your whittling knife?"

"I'm not cutting myself," Thomas said. "I'll get an infection, and Katie will have to take me to the hospital. Going to the hospital for a frivolous reason robs resources from the community."

"It's a finger prick," Daniel said. "I think you'll survive."

Noah said, "I've got M&Ms."

"Where? Can I have one?" Thomas held out his hand.

"For the ghost, moron!"

Thomas asked, "Do ghosts eat M&Ms?"

Sammy cocked his head. He didn't know. "Maybe," he said.

Noah said, "I'm going inside. Who's with me?"

Thomas folded his arms and looked down at his

feet. Sammy took off his glasses and wiped them with his gloves. Daniel farted.

Cowards, all of them. Noah suggested, "Daniel?" He was the latest weakest link.

"I'll walk you to the door. But if it looks like anyone sees us, we run. My daed will have me hauling water from the well for the horses for days if we get caught." There was a spigot outside the barn, but Daniel's daed insisted on the well a quarter-mile from the house for punishments.

He meant it to build character, and it might have, if Daniel hadn't figured out how to pin the blame for most things on his younger brother, who enjoyed going to the well and dreamed of one day becoming an English baseball star.

Tom said, "I'll keep a lookout."

Noah nodded. You couldn't expect more from Thomas. "Sammy?"

Sammy sighed. "To the door. I am not going inside. Bad things happen to people who mess with forces they don't understand."

Sammy ducked between the narrow space between the upper and lower fence slats. Noah and Daniel scrambled over the top, Noah with more sighing and wheezing.

They crossed the yard, hard dirt broken by

rocks and patches of icy snow. To the right of the house was the famous oak where Salome had been buried. They'd taken the ribbons down. Only a shriveled brown leaf hung from one branch. When the breeze blew, the leaf trembled.

Sammy pointed to the now smooth ground at the tree's base. "That's where they found her."

"Big tree," Noah said.

Daniel asked. "Think they left any bones?"

Noah shivered. "Come on." He turned from the tree and walked to the front door. The faster he proved his bravery, the faster he could leave.

They approached the porch. A single note pinged and trailed off.

Daniel jumped. "What's that?"

The wind blew again, rattling the window shutters and sounding two more, lower pitched notes.

"Wind chimes," Noah said, pointing. Someone had hung a set from the awning. Two were broken off, leaving three, one short and two long.

Sammy gasped. He took two steps back, hand shaking as he held it out to the first-floor window. The glass was still in, though it shook in its frame.

"What?" Daniel said, staring at the window.

"Something's in there."

"Where? I don't see anything."

Noah, sensing an opportunity to take Daniel down a peg, said, "I saw it. Like a shadow, but made of smoke."

"No you didn't," Daniel said. "You were looking at the wind chimes, same as me.

"Something moved," Sammy said.

"Maybe it was a rat," Daniel said. "Or a possum. A big fat one."

"It looked like a face."

"We should go," Daniel said.

Daniel was such a coward.

Noah hadn't seen a thing, and Sammy, you never knew where Sammy's imagination would take him. Noah said. "We agreed to go to the door. Unless you're scared. You can go back if you're scared."

"I'm not scared."

"Go ahead. I'm staying here," Sammy said at the base of the steps.

Daniel hesitated. "Maybe Sammy's right."

"Coward."

"I hate you."

"Hate's a sin."

"Shut up."

Noah and Daniel climbed the uneven, chipped concrete stairs onto the porch. The wooden platform beneath their feet was sound and surprisingly clean, with a small pile of dirt settled in one corner.

Daniel shouted down to Sammy, "Looks like somebody swept. Do ghosts sweep up?"

"It would have to be powerful to manifest on the physical plane," Sammy explained.

Noah reached into his pocket and fingered the half-eaten bag of M&Ms he had begged from his mamm on their last weekend trip to the town grocery store. "If Salome's sweeping up, she's considerate." Maybe she was just living there until she moved onto heaven.

Daniel said, "Touch the door."

"Don't do it," Sammy shouted up to them. "You'll wake her up."

"What's she's going to do, sweep us to death?" Daniel laughed.

"*You* touch it," Noah said.

Daniel wouldn't. He talked big, but when it came to action, he curled his nose into his belly like a mealworm.

"I knew you were scared," Daniel said. He took a step towards the door, fingers extended. Daniel was just playing, and he would pull away at the last second, or worse, wave his hand in front of the knob like he had touched it but really hadn't.

Noah knew this, but he had his own pride to protect.

As Daniel leaned closer, dramatic and slowly, Noah doubted himself. What if Daniel touched the door? Then Daniel would be the brave one and Noah second best.

Like a snake, Noah darted in front of Daniel and gripped the knob, turning it. The door opened.

Daniel screamed. Then, covering for himself, he shouted, "Get back Salome!"

Noah clutched the bag of M&Ms. His eyes adjusted to the inside darkness. A small table stood to the right of the open door. The floors were bare, hardwood, a dim hallway leading past a flight of stairs. There weren't even any spider webs. It was just a stupid, boring old house.

Noah laughed, pointing at Daniel. "You screamed."

"You screamed too!"

Had he? "No I didn't."

From below, Sammy said, "Just leave the M&Ms and let's go."

Daniel asked, "Shouldn't someone have locked the door?"

"I bet whoever they hired to clean the place forgot it, last time." Noah said.

Daniel said, "I haven't heard about them hiring anyone to watch the house."

"They had to. It's too clean." Noah had been stupid to be scared. "They'd hired Beanpole to clean the place. And after what happened, you think they would hire another Amishman?"

Daniel shrugged.

Sammy said, "Let's just leave the M&Ms and go.

"Yeah." Daniel nodded, "It's boring here."

Noah smiled. The ghost still scared Daniel. This was Noah's chance. He said, "I'm going inside."

"That's trespassing."

The wind chimes tapped against each other, a discordant tumbling of mismatched notes.

"Tom's keeping watch. And Sammy's out here too. You don't have to go. I'll see if they have a pen and paper and leave a note about the door being unlocked. Is not trespassing if you're trying to help." And Noah would prove, once and for all, that he wasn't scared of ghosts. Or anything else.

Daniel broke. "You go ahead then."

Noah tapped two fingers to his temple in an almost salute. Amishmen weren't supposed to fight in wars, but until Noah had finished his rumspringa, he didn't have to do everything the

Ordnung said. At least when his mamm and daed weren't watching.

Noah crossed the threshold into the house. It was English, so there were switches on the walls but no electricity, so it stayed dark.

They wouldn't use electricity in an empty house.

"What's wrong?" Daniel called near the side of the door.

"Nothing. I was just checking for lights." Noah stepped away from the open door and into the dim hallway. While there were no windows in the hallway, ahead, a dim halo of light glowed from the far back room, which Noah guessed was a kitchen. There might be a pad and paper there. He glanced up the stairs.

At the top, haloed in grayish blue, the silhouette of a woman in Amish dress. She held a stick.

Noah's guts froze.

They said Beanpole had smashed Salome's head in with a heavy stick.

Panicked, Noah grabbed the bag of M&Ms and threw them at the woman. The candied chocolate clattered against the stairs. He turned on his heel and screamed, "Run!" as he dashed for the door.

Laughter. The door slammed shut in front of him.

Daniel. It had to have been Daniel, otherwise it was the ghost, and Noah was about to have the soul sucked out through his ears, and he was a dead kid running. A stupid, dead kid running. Noah grabbed the knob, turned it, and pulled with all of his strength.

From the other side, Daniel taunted. "Scaredy-Noah!"

The English had words Noah wasn't supposed to know, but he used them now. "Let me out! She's here!"

Daniel must have heard the fear in Noah's voice because when Noah pulled again, the door swung free. Daniel and Sammy were down the stairs when Noah got out of the house. He followed them across the yard and through the fence.

Thomas saw them running and took off ahead of them, his boots crunching ice and brambles.

At the edge of the road, Noah gulped heaving breaths as he tapped himself. He'd know if the ghost was inside of him, wouldn't he?

"You saw her?" Sammy asked.

Noah nodded.

The others stood in solemn silence.

"How do I know if she got me?" Noah asked.

Sammy gave a slight nod, pressing his lips

together as he thought. After ten agonizing seconds, he said, "If she isn't in you now, she'll come through your dreams. Most likely. That's how it goes in my brother's books."

"Those aren't real," Noah argued.

Sammy shrugged. "Just be careful. Maybe the Bishop can exorcise you?"

"That's Catholic," Thomas said. "It would be a sin to have a Catholic priest do whatever kind of ritual on you."

Noah thought sinning might be better than getting devoured by an angry ghost. Especially since he hadn't taken his Kneeling Vows.

"Good luck, Noah," Thomas said. "I'm going home. And I'm not going back there, but I'll pray for you tonight."

"Yeah, me too." The others nodded.

Noah said. "I gave her the M&Ms before I ran." More accurately, he had thrown them, but hopefully the offering had been enough either way. "That should be good enough, shouldn't it?"

Sammy adjusted his glasses. "Maybe. If you offered it with a true heart."

With that, the boys continued down the road back to their homes.

1
_____

*K*erosene heaters and the press of bodies offset the chill, so their breath did not ghost the air of the Stoltzfus' barn.

Susie and her daughter Margaret had stopped by the Stoltzfus house to drop off a tray of broccoli and macaroni salad she had made the night before to share. Joseph, Susie's husband, already sat on the men's side of the meeting having an animated conversation with his friend Boaz.

"Is that Greta, looking so tall?" Hannah, newly married and four-months pregnant with her first child, said, kneeling down to meet Margaret's gaze.

Margaret looked at Susie, who smiled. "Go ahead, Greta."

The child's grip on Susie's hand tightened. She nodded, once.

"How old are you?"

"Four," Margaret murmured.

Margaret was not an Amish name. Susie given her daughter the name to keep a promise she and Salome had made as children. The community had shortened it to Greta, some looking up their noses as Susie for naming her daughter the too-long, English form.

"Four!" Hannah exclaimed with exaggerated interest. "You're so big. I bet you'll be a lot of help when your mamm gives you a little brother or sister."

Margaret looked up at Susie who forced a smile. Her blood had come again this morning with a bitter sense of failure. Three years, the last making a serious effort, but no conception.

"We're trying," Susie said.

Hannah averted her gaze. "I'm sorry. I should have thought—"

"It's fine." The only thing worse than the reminder was the apology, flavored with a mix of fear, unconscious superiority, and guilt. "Things will happen in their own time." Her obstetrician wanted to test Susie's eggs and Joe's sperm, and possibly try Susie on some hormone replacement.

Though she hadn't conceived, at least Susie hadn't lost another child. Next to finding Salome's body, miscarrying had been the most painful experience of Susie's life. Would hormone replacement make a miscarriage more likely, as they were interfering with Gott's plan for her conceiving?

Susie didn't know. She desperately wanted another child, but she just didn't know.

Hannah quickly changed the subject, chattering about cakes as they inched closer to a large wooden table, piled high with coats.

Services started on the hour. When they reached the table, Margaret held out her hands, and Susie pulled off her daughter's gloves. Susie had clipped them to a string through the sleeves of the coat, which she pulled her daughter out of next, taking off the hat and shoving it into the sleeve of the girl's English-style winter coat. Margaret put her index and middle finger into her mouth, sucking on them like a child a year younger.

The barn door opened again, letting in another rush of cold air. Hannah's eyes narrowed. Amish people were not demonstrative, so it was jarring when she took Susie's hand. She muttered, "Shame, having him here."

"Beanpole?" Susie wished Hannah had not pointed him out.

"Of course, Beanpole. I do not know how you can stay so composed."

Susie was not composed. Inside, she shook with rage. This was the second church meeting Beanpole had attended since his return from the English institution. It was their way to forgive, but Susie could not forgive the man who had killed her best friend. The best she could do was avoid him.

"I suppose we had to take him back into the community, but the Elders should have asked us," Hannah whispered between her teeth, "They should have asked you."

Conversation around them quieted. Susie felt the gazes of others on her. She had thought seeing Beanpole would get easier. It wasn't, not with Hannah saying exactly what Susie thought.

Hannah was not the only one who had noticed Beanpole at the door between his father, Andrew "Jumbo," Miller and his mamm, Emma, who, since her months in the facility, therapy, and medication, had taken to squeezing a small, orange ball in her right hand to relieve stress.

Beanpole's expression was glazed, his face slack. His hands trembled.

"Mamm?" Margaret lifted her arms so Susie would lift her to see who or what her mamm was staring at.

"Not now," Susie said, averting her gaze. The elders wanted to offer Beanpole a second chance, and who was Susie to argue with them? It was the Amish way to forgive. And Beanpole hadn't meant to hurt Salome. At least that's what he had said. Salome's death had been a tragic accident.

Hannah said, "Forgiveness is all well and good, but we need to keep ourselves safe."

What would Salome say? More than Beanpole, the community's silence had caused Salome's death. Was Susie repeating the same mistake?

The question occupied Susie's mind the entire three-hour service. Beanpole sat on the opposite side of the barn, on the men's side of the service, and close the bishop. Susie stole glances at him. The worst was the devotion Beanpole had shown Salome for so long after he had killed her. Beanpole had loved Salome in his twisted way. He had even, if one believed his confession, tried to save her. The Elders believed him. So had the English judge and the doctors at the institution.

But if Beanpole had loved Salome, if he had tried to save her, then why did Susie hate him so? Hate twisted in Susie's chest like a hot snake, coils rasping. She gritted her teeth, feigning calm as Mr. Schrock, a deacon and Hannah's uncle-in-law, said the final amen.

Through the long morning service, Margaret had fallen asleep with her cheek pressed against Susie's thigh. Susie jiggled it, and Margaret yawned, rubbing her eyes.

"Greta?" Susie said, gently shaking her daughter's shoulder.

Margaret sat up. "I'm hungry," she mumbled.

"I'll take you to Daed and you can stay with him while I help the other women bring in the plates for the Fellowship."

Margaret pointed across the aisle to another young boy, Matt Hoschtetler, who had been born three months earlier than Margaret. They played together sometimes.

Susie smiled, and taking her daughter's hand, walked her over to her friend. The boy's father, Boaz Hoschtetler, was tall and broad, towering over the other men. His upper body was corded muscle from working in the blacksmith trade. A gentle giant with a touch of the clown, he grabbed up his son at the waist and lifted the child over his head. The boy laughed.

Joseph loved playing such games with Margaret, and he would too with a son, if only Susie and her rebellious body could give him one.

Margaret tugged on Susie's dress and pointed. "Please?"

"If you ask nicely," Susie said, knowing Boaz was certain say yes. He loved children and refereed games of pickup baseball and soccer for the boys and girls between their school and rumspringa years. He also chaperoned the rumspringa-aged teens in youth volleyball.

Joseph, catching sight of his wife, finished his conversation and came to her side. It would be odd for him to put his arm around her or kiss her in public, but the warmth of his gaze and the brush of his fingers over the top of her hand as he greeted her showed his affection.

Susie smiled, and the snake of anger she had held tight through the service relaxed. "Husband," she said. "I had hoped—"

"Leave Greta with me."

Their daughter gave a delighted shriek as Boaz swung her up into the air. She held her hands out, palms flat. "Flying!" She giggled.

"Denki." Susie said, wishing for a moment that it was appropriate to kiss her husband on the cheek or slip her arms around his waist in a loving embrace as Tiffany and Malcolm did sometimes when he dropped her and her two children off to meet with Susie in town.

With a final goodbye to Margaret, waiting her turn for Boaz to lift her, Susie went with the other ladies to the Stoltzfus's kitchen to take pans of prepared food back to the barn for the Fellowship.

It was early March, and the air was still winter crisp. Snow dusted the hard-packed ground of the driveway, further out fences, and fallow fields. Though it was too cold to eat outside, the wind was not strong. Susie sorted through the pile of outerwear until she found a coat, slipping it over her shoulders and wrapping her scarf around her neck. She kept her hat and gloves in her pockets. It was a short walk between the barn and the house, and she would not need them on the way back while carrying a hot pan of food.

When Susie reached the kitchen, a knot of women stood by the stove, the rest of the line of ladies stretching into the hall. Mrs. Stoltzfus, just turned 55, managed the kitchen for her guests with the help of her four daughters, ages 11 to 19, who handed out pans of food, dishes and napkins to each woman to return to the barn.

Susie stepped on a stab of jealousy at the sight of Mrs. Stoltzfus's large and happy family. Susie had always wanted a lot of children, and now, four years after Margaret's birth, she prayed her dream was not in vain.

When she reached the stove, Anna, the second oldest girl, sixteen in her first year of rumspringa, handed Susie a glass pan filled with hot cheesy casserole.

Susie took the casserole with a smile, cradling it in the arm of her coat she squeezed past the group back into the hallway. Hannah tapped her arm as she passed. "The men are still setting up the tables. Is Tiffany coming to quilt with us on Tuesday?"

Susie smiled, thinking of her English friend. With two children now, her son Tyrese born after Margaret, and her youngest, Mariah, who had celebrated her first birthday in October, Tiffany did not have much time to investigate mysteries, but she came twice a month for quilting parties, and she had invited Susie and her family over for dinner on a monthly basis, more in the summer. Though it was against the Ordnung for Susie to have air-conditioning in her home, she was not forbidden from appreciating it in others'.

"She said she was, provided there is no emergency at the office with one of her agents." Tiffany was now a real estate broker, which meant she managed a group of real estate agents besides showing and selling her own homes. Though Susie would trade nothing for her life with Joseph, she admired her friend for all of her accomplishments.

And though Susie would not admit it, she was also jealous Tiffany and Malcolm already had a second child.

"Wunderbar! I wrote out the recipe for chocolate chip monkey bread she said she wanted to try."

Susie shook her head. Monkey Bread was sweet enough without adding chocolate chips. Hannah leaned in closer until their shoulders touched and whispered, "Have you truly forgiven him?"

Lying was a sin, and even if it wasn't, lies had hurt too many of the people Susie loved. Susie said nothing.

"Deacon Schrock did not believe we ought to take Beanpole back. If he steps out of line at all..."

Susie nodded. Her throat was thick. "Maybe someone can keep an eye on him."

Hannah nodded. After a few seconds, she said

in a more normal tone, "Greta is getting so tall! Soon she will be able to help you around the house.

Susie smiled. "She is already helping to dry the dishes."

"Sweet child. Quiet. Is she always so quiet at home?"

"Ja. Greta likes to study things. A few months back, she would sit and pour sugar through a funnel into a glass just to watch it fall. She didn't even eat it. Joseph had left the funnel on the table, and Greta climbed up on a chair and pulled the sugar container to her. She had planned it all out."

"She's a smart one."

"Sometimes." Out of politeness, Susie demurred. "I worry she doesn't speak enough. And she's shy around other children."

Hannah said, "She'll come through that. My brother, Thomas, he's the youngest, used to be quiet too. Now, he's always talking and doing things he shouldn't. He broke his arm last year, balancing on a branch next to our barn, trying to jump. One of the other boys dared him to, I bet. And then there's trouble he got into Thursday, with that house—" Hannah said, shaking her head. "Thomas has to be brave. He won't acknowledge his fears, so he's scared all the time and always trying to prove he isn't. Boys."

"I thought bravery was going on in spite of fear," Susie said.

"Ja. But if you don't let yourself feel what you're feeling, you're not overcoming it. You're just pushing through."

Susie murmured agreement before, holding her casserole, she gestured to the door. "I'll see you back at the Fellowship," she said.

"Ja," Hannah agreed, moving towards the kitchen as the line of women moved forward. Susie crossed back to the barn with her pan. Inside, they had pushed the benches against the walls. Three large tables sat in the center aisle between them, laden with foodstuffs. Other women trickled in, and each, like Susie, laid their items on the tables. Susie pulled the tinfoil from the top of her casserole and, taking a serving spoon, dipped it inside.

Task finished, Susie looked around for her husband and daughter. Joseph and Boaz were still talking. Catching his eye, Joseph pointed towards a set of benches on the ladies' side of the barn where three elderly women and a smattering of new grandmothers sat together with a group of children, all under five-years-old.

A pair of new mothers, cradling infants in their arms, sat on the nearest bench chatting with each other. Susie spotted Matthew, Boaz's son. But where was Margaret?

Though Susie did not need to worry for a child in the safety of a barn at church meeting, her heart sped up when she did not see her child around amongst the group. She looked out over the rest of the barn. Was Margaret under one of the benches? She got nervous on her own around large groups of people.

Why hadn't Joseph kept an eye on her? When they had more children, both her and Joseph's responsibilities would increase.

Susie walked back towards the table with the food, thinking Margaret, hungry, might've tried to grab one of the hot, buttery rolls near the table's edge. Hannah had returned and was now chatting with her sister.

Susie did not wish to interrupt. She walked from one end of the barn to the other, looking up and down the benches. "Greta!" Susie called out.

A woman asked, "Your daughter?"

Susie nodded.

"Annie took her and little Katie outside to the chickens."

Little Katie was six. Annie was eleven and capable of minding the child, but the girl should've asked.

Susie, not stopping for her coat, went back outside. A small group of children clustered near the chicken coop. Susie jogged towards them, irritated.

Then her stomach plummeted. Greta stood far from the other children, speaking with a tall, thin man. Though Susie saw him from behind, she knew him.

Beanpole.

Beanpole was speaking with her child!

The snake of fury inside Susie's chest uncoiled, teeth snapping. "Get away from her!" Susie shouted.

Man and child whirled around.

"Margaret! Come here right now."

Wide-eyed, Margaret stood in place, fists clenched. She was terrified, and it was Beanpole's fault. Hadn't the elders warned him to keep away from the children? Beanpole had killed Salome. He did not have a right to speak with the children. He didn't have a right to be here.

Tears stung Susie's eyes. She held her hand out to her child, who wailed.

"Back!" Susie glared at Beanpole.

The man took three steps back, his side brushing the wire fence around the chicken coop. Susie stepped closer to Margaret, hand outstretched. Margaret took it. Her face was red and her cheeks were wet as Susie pulled her back towards the barn.

"It's okay now, Greta," she said, holding fast to her daughter.

"You're hurting me."

Susie swept her child up into her arms. Guilt choked her. Margaret clenched and opened her right fist. Susie had been holding too tightly. "Sorry, I'm so sorry," Susie repeated, pressing a kiss to her daughter's forehead.

Margaret sniffled and then flung her arms around Susie's neck.

Susie returned to the barn, found her husband, and said to him, "We are going home."

"We can't stay here." The elders had forgiven Beanpole, and Susie couldn't cause more of a scene here. Greta had been in full view of the other children and adults by the chicken coop. No edict prevented him from speaking with Margaret. The thought made Susie want to hit Beanpole until she bruised his flesh.

"But the Fellowship?"

"I can't stay here. Not with Beanpole." Though it was against the Ordnung, Susie knew the other women had to be discussing Susie's breakdown at the chicken coop.

"What did he do?"

"Nothing. He was speaking with Margaret, but it isn't forbidden. I can't— Please, can we go now?" Susie couldn't stay. She was too angry.

Joseph sighed and said, "I will have plates made for us. We can return them when we pick up our pan next week."

2
_____

*N*oah spread hay on the floor of the barn. He and his brother, Luke, had finished mucking out the horses, refilling their water troughs and putting out feed. "I promise to Gott! I am not lying. She was there. Salome! And now, what if she is inside of me?"

Luke looked skeptical. "Ghosts are not real."

"Sammy says they are. His brother showed him books about them from the English library. I can't go to sleep. If I do, she will come out and... Do things..."

While Luke did not believe for a moment that his brother was possessed, it was clear the boy did. Dark circles smudged his eyes, and he'd reddened his forearm, pinching it to keep himself awake all night.

"It's not a ghost that has you like this. Whatever your friend said, it's wrong. Put your trust in Gott. He will protect you. He protects all of us."

"Gott will protect *you*," Noah said. "You're going to take your Kneeling Vows, and even if you didn't, you follow the Ordnung to the letter. I'm not so good. Even when I try. There are plenty of holes in me for sin to leak through. And that's how *she's* going to get me."

"There is no *she*. I will go and prove it."

Noah grabbed Luke's hand. "No! You can't!"

"I can and I will. I'll borrow grandma's iron horseshoe and some salt." While it was important, above all things, to put one's faith in Gott, the iron horse shoe had its own sort of power which Luke and Noah believed in implicitly. "And when I come back and there is no ghost, you'll stop this foolishness and take a nap?"

"I'm not scared," Noah said. "I can go with you."

Luke, knowing how important it was to his little brother to 'not be scared', shook his head. "I need you here in case Daed asks where I've gone. Lying is a sin, so just tell him I stepped out to deal with something, and I'll be back. You don't have to say what."

Noah agreed, and so it was Luke, on the Monday afternoon after church services, who went to take care of the ghost. Or *not* the ghost, which was most likely.

But before visiting the ghost, Luke went to his grandmother's room. The elderly woman napped in her chair in front of the window. Luke took the horseshoe with a mumbled apology and made his way to the old Crawley house.

Everyone said it was haunted, but Luke knew better than to believe that. Still, Luke shivered as he stared out over the yard, his gaze flitting to the tree underneath which Beanpole had buried Salome.

The horseshoe was heavy in his right pocket. Luke gripped it, steadied by its cold weight. The faster he got this done, the faster he could return and tell his brother to stop letting Sammy's brother's horror novels leak into their real world.

Luke scrambled over the fence and walked towards the house. The English service the Crawleys' had hired to maintain the grounds was doing an excellent job. They scrubbed the front stairs and swept the porch, and while one shutter had come open, lazily tapping the house's outer wall, the window behind it was clear.

Noah had said the door was unlocked, but when Luke tried it, the knob didn't turn.

Considering how clean and organized the grounds looked, it was likely someone had come in over the weekend to take care of the place. If so, they should have closed the shutter. Luke circled the house, stopping at the back door which led to the kitchen from a set of old, wooden stairs. If Luke could not get in through this door, he would tell Noah he had not seen the ghost and hopefully it would be enough to assuage his imaginative younger brother.

Stepping carefully—Luke did everything care-fully—he climbed the stairs. To his dismay, the back door opened easily. He stepped inside, clicking a battery-powered flashlight and letting the beam sweep over the room.

No ghost. No surprise either. The room smelled of cigarette smoke, which surprised Luke. An ashtray with three spent butts sat on the kitchen counter.

Luke's estimation of the Englishers maintaining this house dropped. Stupid Beanpole, burying a body here, and thus leaving local jobs to slovenly Englishers.

Luke wiped his palm over his forehead. He walked to the sink and looked inside. The sink was bifurcated. On the left side, someone had placed a bucket, empty and upside down. On the right sat two dishes, plain white crockery, and a fork with one tine bent backwards. They were clean at least.

Luke, irritated, opened one of the cabinets. It was empty. He placed the plate inside. Then he opened a drawer. It was empty except for a pack of cigarettes and a bent spoon. He put the fork beside the spoon.

As Luke performed these tasks, the oddness of the situation struck him.

What business did English cleaners have with keeping a chipped plate, a fork and spoon in an empty house? Luke opened the second set of cabinets. Inside sat a line of canned goods. Beans. Peaches.

Noah had claimed to have seen a woman holding a large stick.

Luke did not believe in ghosts, but it was possible someone was squatting here.

But whoever it was had dressed as an Amish

woman. Could a girl from the neighboring community have run away? And if so, why here?

Luke felt awkward, rifling around a strange girl's home. But if she was squatting here, she would be cold at night. Cold canned beans and peaches would provide little comfort. Did she have a flashlight? Lantern?

A blanket?

The proper thing to do would be to report her to the bishop or a deacon and have them contact the owners of the house. But just this once, Luke did not wish to do the proper thing. He had no true evidence the girl was squatting here. It was just a suspicion.

Luke's thoughts drifted towards the tree, and the young woman who had been buried there. She had suffered at home. Luke's mother had whispered of it, how Salome Beiler's daed had partaken of the fruit of the vine and was too rough with his children. No one spoke of it. No one wished to know. So it was only whispers.

Perhaps this girl had been drawn here for the same reason? She couldn't have been here long. Someone checked on this house. Maybe not as often as he'd thought, but they would check in, eventually. Until then, if a girl was hiding here,

Luke couldn't drive her away. Better she stayed here than find herself in worse trouble.

Maybe he could make her life a little easier. Give her things. A blanket. Some better food. If he proved himself a friend, she might come out and tell him why she'd run away.

It was not to the letter of the Ordnung. But, maybe, for once, he did not wish to be Luke who always did what he was supposed to do. Man of the house at eleven upon his father's heart attack. Reliable. Boring. Even his own girlfriend has left him because he was too dull and correct.

Now Sadie courted with Mark, and Luke, ordinary, boring Luke, had no one.

Luke returned to the cabinet, took the bowl out and placed it back in the sink, putting the fork atop it. He would return with blankets and some of his mamm's famous cauliflower and cheese roast.

And another blanket and a pillow. His family had extras for guests.

Luke's thoughts whirled as he hurried across the yard. Wind blew, shaking the oak and causing the wind chimes to echo a haunted, discordant tune.

3
_____

our women, three Amish and one English, sat in Katie Troyer's living room, thick needles in hand, patchwork quilt squares draped around them. The house smelled of sanded wood and a baking pot roast in the oven.

Tiffany, respectful of her friends' modesty although they did not require her to share it, wore a long black skirt and silver, long-sleeved blouse with a heavy, zippered sweatshirt over it. Her gloves had the fingers cut off, and she wore a second, dark blue scarf tied around her coiled curls.

The ladies had spread a large quilt on the floor for the children. Mariah sat in the middle and banged a pair of Tupperware containers together, occasionally smacking them with a length of tied-together quilt straps braided and knotted so the toddler would not chew on them and choke.

Tyrese and Margaret sat on the edge of the blanket, building something with blocks. Katie's daughter, four months old, slept in a bassinet next to her mother on the couch.

Katie was a slight woman with quick, darting hands. She asked, "Have any of you noticed clothing gone from the lines?"

Susie shook her head.

Hannah asked, "What sorts of clothes? Not... Your underthings?"

There had been a scandal a few years back where an English man had stolen Amish ladies' underthings from the drying lines in Indiana. It had made all the Amish papers, and for a year, ladies had either dried their underthings as best they could inside or, on rare occasions, pulled together to rent a driver to taken their underclothing to a laundromat.

Katie shook her head. "Ne! Ne! A dress and an apron. It was one of my old ones, before the baby. And I was thinking I could wear it again soon. Or give it to my niece."

"Are you sure your husband didn't take it inside?"

Katie shook her head. "No. The other clothes around the dress were still there. Only the dress was missing."

"That's odd," Hannah said. "I heard the Fishers had a ruckus in their henhouse in the middle of the night three nights ago." Hannah shook her head. "And…" She shook her head again. "It sounds stupid, but she also said, come the next morning, she was missing some rolls she had left to cool on the oven."

"Maybe we have a vagrant," Susie said. "Has anyone spoken with the bishop? Or one of the deacons?"

Hannah said, "I spoke to my uncle. We cannot have strange men creeping in our homes, stealing our things."

"In Christian charity," Katie said, "I would not begrudge the hungry a roll or an egg."

"I would begrudge them my underthings," Hannah muttered. "Shirt off of your back is one thing, but…"

"It wasn't underwear," Katie protested.

"Are you sure? Have you counted them?"

"I'm sure," Katie said, but she averted her gaze, turning to the peacefully sleeping infant as though the girl had cried out.

Susie said, "It might not have been a vagrant in the henhouse. Just as likely it was a weasel. Or a fox."

"Whatever it was," Hannah said, her mouth set in a firm, downward hooked line, "Something must be done. There are children." She grazed her palm over her belly. The baby hadn't begun to show, but she protected it even so.

Mariah crawled over to the tower of blocks. Rolling onto her rear, she reached for one.

Tyrese shouted, "No!"

But it was too late. Mariah grabbed the topmost block and shoved it into her mouth. The other blocks teetered. Margaret grabbed for the structure, trying to hold it in place. It fell in a loud clatter. Tyrese glared at Mariah. "Baby!"

Mariah burst into tears. Margaret held out her arms to Mariah, patting her on the shoulder. After a few moments, Tyrese came around her other side and patted her back. "It's all right," he murmured, though he glanced back at the fallen blocks and sighed.

"They're sweet at that age," Katie said. "I remember my little brother…"

Susie said, "If a fox is stealing eggs, people should know to look out for it. A fox is dangerous."

The other women nodded.

Hannah said, "What if it was Beanpole?" Her tone was hushed.

"Stealing eggs?" Katie looked up.

"Ne! Stealing ladies' clothing. He took his mamm's old clothes when he was... Keeping house... With Salome."

Tiffany asked, "Do you think Beanpole would kidnap somebody?"

Susie shivered. "Nobody else has disappeared," she said.

Katie laughed, but the sound had a higher pitch than joyful laughter. "The elders would not have let him back into our district if they thought he was dangerous. We have to trust in their wisdom."

Hannah said, "My brother Noah was whispering to some of his friends. They say the Crawley place is haunted."

Katie snorted. "Of course, they say it's haunted. No offense to you Susie, but they know Beanpole buried Salome there. And even if he hadn't, the place is so long abandoned, and boys are boys. Old houses are always haunted, don't you know?"

Susie could not argue with this logic. As much as she wanted Beanpole to be guilty of something— not kidnapping or murdering again—but something that would force the elders to cast him out once and for all, he wasn't allowed anywhere near the Crawley house anymore.

All three children were playing with the blocks again, stacking them, though Mariah's coordination, at just over a year of age, meant she collapsed more than she built.

Tiffany held out a square of purple and gold patterned fabric. It was not an Amish design. She had picked up the squares at an African festival in the city. Susie wished the strictures of her Ordnung allowed her to use such a bright, merry pattern in her own work. Tiffany asked, "I have enough for five squares, I think. Where would it be best to place them?"

After some consultation, the women returned to their stitching. After a few minutes, Tiffany pulled her quilt up higher on her lap and clenched her hands around it. "I have news," she said with a shaky smile.

Cold fear spiked Susie's guts. Was Tiffany leaving Lancaster? She had shown all signs setting down roots, but Englishers often followed their jobs. If Malcolm had found a better income elsewhere, then they might be all preparing to leave, no matter the success of Tiffany's real estate brokerage. Real estate, as Tiffany had often said, was a pack up and go career.

Tiffany looked down at her hands. "We wanted to wait until after the first trimester..."

Hannah squealed. "Another boppoli!"

"We don't know if it is a boy or girl—"

"A healthy boppoli is all that matters!" Katie declared.

All three women gathered around Tiffany, offering their congratulations. Susie forced a smile. "I thought you seemed tired."

"The morning sickness isn't as bad as with Mariah. I'm thinking it's a boy. Tyrese was easier at the beginning too."

Susie was happy for her friend, but it high-lighted Susie's inability to conceive another child. She and Joseph had been trying for over three years now.

The English doctor had suggested they speak with a specialist, but Susie was reluctant to circum-vent Gott's will with artificial fertility treatments. There had to be something else she and Joseph could do. Stress could make it more difficult for Susie to conceive, the doctor had told her.

Maybe Susie's fear of another miscarriage was causing the trouble. Or maybe Gott had other plans for Susie. Or maybe it was Beanpole? She couldn't forgive him, and now, as the Elders had allowed him back, she had to deal with him far too often.

Susie couldn't forget Beanpole's attempt to "befriend" Margaret. His presence in the community put them in danger. How could she bring another child into the community with Beanpole free to do as he wished?

As women discussed a new baby quilt for Tiffany's soon to be third born, Susie gave the conversation only half of her attention. Something had to be done about Beanpole. And herself.

Something had to be done.

4

$\mathcal{M}$ aryanne had never worked so hard or smelled so bad in her entire life. Her brown hair was pulled back in a messy bun, her lips were chapped, her hands cracked from washing her "borrowed" clothes in the gas station bathroom a half-hour walk away with a bar of harsh white soap she found at the back of the cabinet beneath the sink.

It was harder out here in the country, but there were benefits to having her own place, even if it lacked electricity, heat, or running water. Maryanne didn't have to worry about a friend's parents getting tired of her on their couch. She didn't have to worry about people stealing her stuff if she fell asleep.

Most importantly, she didn't have to worry about cops tracking her. She'd been stupid to call the cops on her cell phone. Now they knew her name. Now, as she'd feared, they suspected she had something to do with Mr. Timothy Eldridge's murder.

How much longer could Maryanne hide here before Tim became old news?

Maryanne glanced out the kitchen window. The sun had risen an hour ago, which meant the Amish guy would visit. With breakfast. That was the best thing about living here. Him. She didn't even know his name. She'd been too scared at first to come out and tell him, 'thank you.'

I really am the worst.

Maryanne really needed, at least, to thank him. He wouldn't know about Tim. The Amish didn't watch the news, and besides, people were shot and killed every day in Philly.

The Amish guy looked her age, maybe a year older, and he had visited every morning to leave her gifts.

A sandwich. Slices of thick, gooey cinnamon bread. He left cold sweet tea in a large water jug, which she washed out every evening so he could take it from the sink and refill it.

After an evening so cold she'd shivered even in her winter coat, hat, boots, and gloves, her Amish benefactor had delivered three heavy quilts, a pillow and two dog-eared comics.

Maryanne didn't even like superhero comics, with their large breasted, scantily clad women and men built like slabs of beef. But the Amish boy, tall, wide shouldered, and with a narrow waist like the characters he seemed to favor, was a hero to her, and she wanted to know more about him. She needed to thank him.

Also, though Maryanne did not want to admit it to even herself, she was lonely and bored. She had thought living on the run would involve more excitement and less hauling buckets of water up from the creek to flush the toilet. Less canned beans.

Maryanne owed her Amish hero. If it wasn't for him, she might have turned herself in to spare herself the hunger and cold.

In anticipation of meeting her Amish friend, Maryanne had sprayed herself with discount pharmacy perfume. *Island breeze.* She considered a touch of lipstick, but Amish guys didn't go for girls with makeup, did they?

Maryanne had seen a movie about the Amish

people, and once, when her aunt had gotten out of rehab and been clean for a month, they had gone to the big market and she saw women in aprons and bonnets like the one she had found in the upstairs bedroom.

The Amish didn't go for stealing either, so Maryanne already had a strike against her. She slipped the lipstick back into her purse.

Now all she had to do was wait.

The sun had come up, and she stood out of view of the back kitchen door, her back to the hallway wall.

Maryanne rubbed her thumbs together and tried to dampen her excitement. Finally, she heard the familiar tread of booted feet climbing over the wooden stairs and the creak of the kitchen door.

Maryanne flattened herself against the wall and tried not to breathe.

"Hello!" called the Amish boy, except by the broadness of his shoulders, his height, and the hint of a razor burn on his jaw, he was not a boy. In Maryanne's before life, she'd say he was a guy, an Amish guy.

The Amish guy always knocked before he entered, which made Maryanne smile. It wasn't like she lived here. Okay, so she was living here, but it wasn't like she had *permission* to live here.

Maryanne's Amish hero carried two paper bags, a tinfoil wrapped package, and a glass bottle of sweet tea.

Maryanne's mouth watered, and her stomach rumbled. Thankfully, he kept up a steady monologue that overwhelmed the small sounds she may have made.

The Amish guy wasn't hot in a way she would have noticed in her regular life. His jaw was too square, his eyes set too wide part, and he had a patch of acne on his right temple. A fall of reddish brown hair obscured the latter, full and wavy. She couldn't guess his eye color, but his lips were full, and his chin had a slight divot she found endearing.

"Miss, I am putting these small things on the table here. Ja?" The 'ja' often punctuated his words. She guessed it meant 'yeah' or "right."

The Amish spoke another language, didn't they? Pennsylvania Dutch.

"Ja, some friends and I will have a Sing tonight. I will be late tomorrow because I will not have work. I can just take this..." He walked to the sink and picked up the plastic jug he had left for her earlier this week. She'd washed it in the creek, closer than the gas station, and left it to dry in the sink.

"Goodbye then," he said, turning to the door.

Maryanne's heart pounded. It scared her to speak, but she couldn't let him leave again. Not without saying something.

"Wait!" Maryanne shouted. She stepped away from the wall.

He dropped the jug, and it thunked in the sink basin.

Maryanne screamed.

"Sorry." He added something else in the rush of Pennsylvania Dutch, or whatever he was speaking.

Maryanne stared at him.

After a few seconds, he said, "You don't understand. I'm sorry."

"Thank you. For the food."

"You like it? My mamm makes the sandwiches, and my sister Hannah baked the Monkey Bread. It's my grandmamm's specialty, from Indiana, and Hannah learned how to make it when we visited five years ago. You're not Amish, are you?"

Maryanne shook her head. "My name is…" She couldn't give her real name, but she hated lying to him, not that she hadn't been lying all along. And squatting. But there were standards. She said, "My name's Marion. Like maid Marion. So I guess that makes you my Lancelot."

It was his turn to stare at her. The Amish kept themselves apart from other people. They didn't even have electricity, or at least that's what she'd heard. "You've never heard of King Arthur and the roundtable?"

"Yes—! No."

"It's okay. I like the comics. Thank you."

"I mean, I know about King Arthur," he said. "My name is Luke. But you can call me Lancelot, if you want. I read the stories."

Maryanne said. "Luke is a nice name." Like Luke Skywalker, the Jedi Knight, but she didn't expect him to know anything about that, and she didn't want to embarrass him again. "I was… Um… I'm just staying here for a while."

"I thought so," Luke said.

They stared at each other, neither wishing to address the obvious. Maryanne had no relationship to the owner of this house. She had no business pretending to live here. And Luke knew it. He was helping her anyway. Why, Maryanne wanted to know but did not know how to ask. Maryanne, wishing to offer him something honest, said, "I'm from Philly."

"My mamm used to sell stuff at the market. But that was years ago. Do you like the city?" Luke shrugged. "Probably not, I guess."

"It's okay."

"Well..."

"You've got to go." Of course he did. Maryanne had already imposed too much on Luke. She still didn't know why he had helped her, and she would not ask. She needed his help.

Luke asked, "Is there anything else you need?"

Maryanne shook her head, the perfume and her own sweat mingling, making her stomach churn. She wrinkled her nose. "A shower."

Way to go, Maryanne. She was terrible at not imposing. How long had he been bringing her food? Five days, maybe a week? She'd lost track of time. Now she was driving him away, or worse, he'd tell someone about her.

Maybe she should just go back to Philly and tell them what she'd seen. Except she'd seen the mayor's son *kill* someone. He was probably looking for her too, to shut her up.

No, better to stay hidden. Before her parents and brother had died, Maryanne had wanted to skip college and go to California to see if she could make it in the movies. She could do that now, just keep going west. If she had more than eight dollars to her name.

Luke said, "We have showers at the mechanic. Did you need a job?"

"Really?"

"It's stupid."

"No! Yes! I mean, I need a job." Maryanne smiled and nodded with vigor. Luke really was her hero. "But I don't know anything about cars. I mean, I don't even have a learner's permit."

"You need not drive. Mr. Johnson needs someone for the front desk. And you'll be able to use the shower. You can come with me today. Jerome's got room for one more in the car, if you sit in the back, in the middle."

5

*H*annah and Susie followed Tiffany to her minivan. She had stopped for both women and their quilting, as usual. Tiffany always made kind gestures like this. She had even bought a second child seat for Margaret, now strapped in next to Tyrese. The quilting materials were in the trunk while Hannah agreed to ride the third row back.

Tiffany backed up from the driveway. Though Susie lived closer to Katie's than Hannah, Tiffany drove to Hannah's first. While Hannah had taken her Kneeling Vows, and none could now doubt her devotion to their faith for the Ordnung, it was clear she missed pop music, and she sang along with the radio in Tiffany's car.

When the station moved to commercials, Hannah shouted, "Do you think it was just Katie? Who got robbed?"

Robbed seemed like a strong term. Susie shrugged.

Tiffany said, "Maybe you should talk to the police. I know Amish folks like to handle things your own way, but if you have a vagrant, you never know if he could turn dangerous."

"We can't go to the police over one dress," Susie said. "Not days after the fact."

"Maybe we can investigate," Hannah said. "Like you did with Salome."

"This is nothing like Salome," Susie snapped.

"I'm sorry," Hannah said, her voice softening. "I only meant to help."

"It's fine."

The worst of it was, Susie wanted to investigate. She wanted to ask questions and find out if Beanpole was involved. The Ordnung admonished against gossip, but this prohibition didn't stop ladies from sharing news. Joe had an order for horseshoes to fulfill with one of Katie's neighbors, Mrs. Annie Fisher, on Friday. Mrs. Fisher was approaching sixty and prone to colds. Susie could accompany Joe and bring soup.

Mrs. Annie Fisher lived to share news.

"I only said something because Katie lives close to Beanpole Miller."

Tiffany clicked on the turn signal and pulled her steering wheel to the right. "I thought your people were keeping an eye on Beanpole. Didn't the judge find Salome's death accidental manslaughter?"

Susie nodded. "And Beanpole repented. The elders have forgiven him. We turn the other cheek." No matter how many times they were struck. Susie recognized this as a pillar of their faith, and she hated her own doubts. But she could not deny them.

Hannah said, "Susie is the best of us."

Tiffany said, "I could not ask for a better friend."

Was Susie a better friend? Salome's bones beneath the Crawleys' tree made a lie of Tiffany's words. If Susie had been a better friend, she could have saved Salome. Susie clutched her hands.

They let Hannah off in front of her home. The minivan door closed automatically behind her. As she pulled out, Tiffany said, "I'm sorry. I had wanted to tell you before. You and Joe have been trying so hard, but I just— I didn't want to hurt you. I know it's not an excuse."

Susie blinked, her throat was thick. She said, "I am thrilled for you. And Malcolm. Joe and I are seeing the doctor next week. We had tests done." Susie had hated them. Dr. Ambrose had checked her eggs and Joseph's sperm, and it all felt far too intrusive. If it was Gott's will she had another child, then she should accept the blessing, and if it was His will she didn't, then she should accept that.

"Any news?"

"Dr. Ambrose prefers to go over things in person." It didn't mean bad news. The doctor had been clear about that when she set the follow-up appointment.

"I'm sure everything will be fine. Margaret is so healthy."

Susie smiled. "She is. Quiet though."

"If I could be so blessed. They say boys talk less but..." Tiffany laughed, glancing back in the rearview mirror at the two children, Tyrese chattering away while Margaret nodded and pulled her ear. Tyrese laughed.

Tiffany said, "Will you talk to Joanne? When my mom died...she helped a lot. And she works with Plain communities. There's no shame in getting a little help."

"I pray," Susie said.

"And you should. But as my grandmother always said, 'sometimes God works by his own hand and sometimes through the hands of others.'"

Tiffany put on her blinkers and, taking a Post-It pad from the glove compartment, wrote the therapist's name and number. Joanne Hudson. A string of numbers. Susie's heart pounded as she put the slip of paper into the pocket in her coat. "Denki," she said, ducking her head.

Susie and Tiffany hugged. It was an English gesture, and while at first it had been awkward as Tiffany was not her husband or blood family, but Tiffany had become family through these years.

After saying goodbye to Tyrese and Mariah, Susie took her quilting from the trunk and unbuckled Margaret, lifting her to the ground. Mother and daughter waved at the minivan as it backed out, executing a three-point turn and pulling back onto the road.

Only after they ate dinner and Margaret was put to bed, did Susie think again about the number of the therapist Tiffany had left. And Tiffany's news.

She and Joseph sat together on the sofa, him reading.

Joseph said, "You're quiet tonight."

"Do you—?" Susie swallowed, squeezing her eyes shut and then opening them. She couldn't look at him. "Are you happy...? Here... With me...? With our lives?"

"Susie Zook," Joseph took her hand and pulled it. "Look at me."

She did. He gazed into her eyes. His hands were calloused from his work in the carpentry shop. "I love you. I love Margaret. You— I know you've been unhappy."

"I'm not unhappy."

"About Beanpole. And I know you want us to have another child."

"Tiffany's pregnant."

A sharp intake of breath. "That's—! That's wonderful news."

Susie's eyes welled up. She blinked tears onto her cheeks. "It is. I am happy for her. I am."

"It's gutt. Very gutt."

"A third boppoli. It is so wonderful. I wanted us to have a large family too." Susie sobbed.

Joseph pulled her into his arms. "Large or small, this is our family. I would not want another."

How could Joseph be so wonderful? Susie was blessed. Too blessed. She wanted to be worthy of him. But even as she was held in the warmth of his arms, surrounded by his love, a shard of cold sat in Susie's chest. It was like a poison, leaching the joy from her life and leaving her empty.

Joseph's arms were around her, but she felt far away. Unreal. As though she looked down upon a ghost of herself.

Maybe she needed to talk to somebody.

That night, curled up in bed beside her husband, Susie dreamed of picking berries with Salome and the race they ran. Salome took off before as she said "race you," allowing her a leg or more head start. But this time, chest burning, legs pumping, Susie slammed past Salome, their shoulders knocking together.

Salome stumbled.

Susie, gleeful at besting her friend for once, kept running towards the rock Salome had declared the finish line. It grew as Susie leaped onto it. Hands bleeding, she scrabbled to hold on, toes pushing at the rock's side for a foothold.

Behind Susie, Salome screamed. Susie looked back. Beanpole stood beside her friend with a large branch gripped between his two hands.

Terrified, Susie shouted for Beanpole to stop,

but it was too late. Salome lay broken on the ground. Beanpole stood over her, his face blank, the branch wrapped in red ribbons.

Susie fell.

Joseph snorted and rolled over, resting his hand on Susie's shoulder.

Susie thought again of the English therapist. To help with his father's business, Joseph had installed a phone in the barn. This late at night, Susie would not need to speak with a receptionist. She could leave a message. Then, in the light of day, when they called back, she could decide.

Susie sat up.

Joseph murmured in his sleep, and Susie patted his hand. "It's okay," she whispered. "I'll be right back."

Standing, Susie donned her robe and slippers and shuffled into the hallway. Her boots were by the door beneath the hook with their coats. The Post-It was still in her coat pocket.

She put on her coat and boots and strode across the dark-field to the barn.

Inside, she picked up the phone and listened as a dial tone sounded. One horse stamped the ground. The air smelled of straw and manure. She dialed the number, but as it rang, her hand shook.

You've reached the office of—
Susie slammed the phone into the cradle.

6

*L*uke said, "Marion is not an Amish name, how about I call you Mary?"

Maryanne nodded. She would be conspicuous as an Amish woman with a non-Amish name. Mary was an ordinary name. Nothing to see here. Luke really was brilliant.

Maryanne and Luke stood together alongside a cornfield to a two-lane road. Luke wore a digital watch on his left wrist. It was large, the face pale yellow with easy-to-read numbers. Maryanne wished she could bring her phone and charger, but you could be tracked by your cellphone, which is why she'd kept it off after she saw her name on the news.

Besides, Amish girls didn't carry cell phones.

She didn't think they used digital watches either. Maryanne really didn't know much about the Amish, which was bad as she was pretending to be one.

Luke said, "I will have to tell Jerome I'm courting with you. He's my coworker and a friend. He started picking up when he heard I had to walk two miles every morning to meet up with the other guys and chip in for a driver."

"You're not allowed to get a license?"

Luke shook his head. "I can if I want to, for now. And a car even. I'm working on restoring a classic VW bug. But when I take my Kneeling Vows, I can't drive anymore."

"Do you have to take them?"

"Ne! I could leave and live as an Englischer, but I can't abandon my family." Luke scratched his cheek. "My daed passed on when I was eleven, and there's still three of us. I'm the oldest."

Mary and put her hand on his arm. "That must be hard," she said.

Luke shrugged. "Mr. Johnson said he's looking for someone to help at the main desk. Can you run a computer?" Luke shook his head. "Of course you can. You're English."

Maryanne said, "I've never worked a job like

this before. I did acting before— I used to act. I was in a cereal commercial once." Beary, beary berries. She'd remember that line until she died. "And I almost got to be Detective Emmy's best friend on her show. It only went one season."

Luke shrugged. "Do you like acting?"

"Yeah." Maryanne said. "I'm going to go to California and be in the movies. I mean, that's what I wanted. Before..." Before her parents died. Before Billy and running away from her aunt's. Before Bobby and Tim.

Maryanne looked down at the ground. She hoped Luke didn't ask about before. If he did, she'd have to lie to him again, and she didn't want to do that.

Thankfully, instead, Luke asked, "What else do you like?"

"I'm no good at anything else."

"That can't be true. I bet you're good at a lot of things."

Why did Luke have to be so nice? She shouldn't be dragging him even further into her mess. She shouldn't have mentioned the shower.

Maryanne forced a smile. She was good at forcing smiles. "I'm just being dramatic. Ignore it. Maybe they will hire me. It'll be fun." She was sixteen, so she wouldn't need her parents' permission to work. Hopefully just putting in her information for taxes wouldn't set off any alarms. Maybe she could transpose two of the numbers when she filled out the form. Then if anyone asked, she could say she made a mistake.

Maryanne should have been more nervous, but in her Amish disguise, clutching a brown paper bag, with Luke beside her, Maryanne felt safe. No one would see a possible murder suspect in the Amish girl standing by the side of the road.

Here, she was just Mary. An empty page.

"Where did you get the comics?" Maryanne asked. "They looked old."

"They were my dad's," Luke explained. "He shouldn't have them anymore, but he kept them in a trunk in the attic. And when I was nine, I found them. I hid up there, reading them after school before he came back from his shop."

"What kind of shop?"

"He did carpentry. I learned a little before…" Luke shook his head. "I'd have liked to study more, but then he passed, and my mamm needed my help on the farm and then…"

"My dad passed too." Maryanne said. "Last year."

"Oh." He put a hand on her shoulder.

"My mom and brother too."

"You're all alone?" He sounded so sympathetic, Maryanne wanted to cry. But tears didn't help anything. Neither did screaming.

Keep your head down and mind your own business.

The landscape might be different but the rule was the same.

"My dad collected comics," Maryanne said. "He wouldn't let anyone read them though." He kept them in neat plastic sheets in his office, on the shelf. She'd never been interested enough to do more than flip through and look at the covers, once, when he was away at work. Now, she wished she'd looked at them more carefully. She wished she hadn't taken him, mom and even Billy for granted. She wished she'd gone with them. Then they'd have all gone together when the truck hit.

A navy Prius slowed as it approached, peeling off towards the shoulder.

Luke said, "That's Jerome."

It pulled up in front of them. Behind the wheel was a tall brown man with close-cropped hair and a gold stud in his right ear. He wore jeans and a heavy denim work shirt.

Luke opened the back door and waved

Maryanne inside. She sat, and he closed the door before slipping into the passenger seat.

"Jerome, this is Mary."

"Good to meet you," Jerome said. His forehead and one eyebrow were visible in the rearview mirror. "You two get back together?'

Luke had dated a girl named Mary?

"Ne!" Luke shifted in his chair. "That was Sadie."

"My bad, Mary." He looked back at her and smiled before turning back to the wheel and clicking the turn signal on.

Luke said, "Mary wants to apply for the office work job."

"She can use a computer?"

Maryanne said, "Yes. Basic stuff." What would an Amish girl say? She'd be modest. Or maybe shy. Maryanne added, "Not well, but I can try."

Jerome nodded and pulled the car back onto the road.

What was Maryanne thinking, going to Luke's workplace and looking for a job? She was hiding out. At the same time, she needed money. And maybe as an Amish girl, she wouldn't have to produce documentation. They wouldn't expect her to have a driver's license. Maybe not a social security number either. Didn't Amish people have home births?

Maryanne didn't have much to lose. She'd just be an Amish girl. One of hundreds around here. Being Amish was a special shield. Nobody would look further than the dress and head covering.

Jerome asked, "How did the two of you meet?"

Maryanne clasped her hands on her lap. She laughed, stupidly. "It's a hilarious story…"

Luke joined in, "Ja! She's… Um… We met in a house my little brother thought was haunted."

Was that why the boy had run away, screaming "She's here?"

Luke's brother had thrown a package of M&Ms behind him. She'd spent ten minutes after he left cleaning them up. And maybe eating a few. Two second rule, which in this case had been more like minutes, but who was counting? She'd gotten less picky about things since becoming a squatter.

"It was embarrassing," Maryanne said. "How was I supposed to know he'd think I was a ghost? I was holding a broom! But I guess with the skylight above me, I looked scary."

Jerome chuckled. Why did your brother think the house was haunted?"

"Nobody lived there," Maryanne said. "And you know how kids are."

"Yeah. My little sister wouldn't go in the closet for a week after staying over her friend's house for a sleepover. Her friend's older sister told them all kinds of crazy stories about aliens or something. Or maybe they saw a movie. I don't know. Moms was pissed."

Maryanne laughed.

Luke said, "Yeah. Noah's friend Sammy's always getting horror books from his older brother. They were scared to death about parasites last month. Some spoor got mutated in a horse, and Noah kept sneaking into the barn to stare down our horses to show he wasn't scared. Noah's more scared of being scared than anything."

"Yeah, I've met your brother."

"You can't even *act* like you're going to dare him to do anything," Luke said.

Jerome asked, "What were you doing in the haunted house, Mary?" His gaze flicked towards Mary in the rearview mirror.

Maryanne gave her sunniest smile. "Cleaning," she said.

Jerome asked, "Was someone paying you?"

Maryanne shook her head.

"You Amish folks are something else, cleaning up houses for free," Jerome said. "No offense."

Mary wasn't sure why it would offend her.

"I see your mom got rid of the plastic bag full of bottles of the back of the car." Luke waved his hand towards the back seat.

Jerome nodded sheepishly. "Good thing too. Otherwise your girl would think I was a slob."

"Wouldn't want her to think that." Luke said, his tone sarcastic.

Maryanne laughed.

Jerome punched Luke in the shoulder. "Not all of us scrub down our workstation and our tools between every break."

"I like to keep things organized."

In the rearview mirror, Jerome's gaze flitted towards Maryanne. "Luke's a keeper. Just saying."

Mary smiled. "I bet he is," she said.

The back of Luke's neck flushed. "We're not yet courting."

Maryanne looked down at her hands. Courting? What an old-fashioned way to talk about dating. Maryanne liked it. Luke didn't look at her like he was just thinking about how to get into her pants. Or up under her dress, considering. He came to the house every morning with food, small essentials, and even a blanket, without knowing what she looked like. And now he was bringing her into his workplace so she could take a shower and pretend she knew how to run Microsoft Office.

Maryanne had been lucky so far, but she couldn't stop worrying about when her luck would run out.

Jerome asked, "Are you sure you want to work for Eddie?"

"Me?"

"Luke, you didn't warn her?"

Maryanne asked, "Warn me about what?"

"Eddie. Mr. Johnson. He can't stand having anyone mess around with his files. Which is why people quit, and he won't throw anything away. He has files from the 70s in his back office. And the computer an antique too. One of those big square monitors and the operating system is from 1997."

Mary blinked. "He doesn't have the money to upgrade?"

"No. He does fine. Sends his wife and kid to Florida for a month every summer. He just doesn't like change." Jerome glanced at Maryanne. "You're Amish though, so I guess you get that."

Mary nodded, even though she wasn't, and she didn't.

Jerome said, "Also, he will try hiring you under the table, if he hires you at all. Eddie can't stand having the government mixed up in his business. He pays on time though, and after a few months, he'll put you on the payroll regular."

Maryanne's heart leapt. If Luke's boss wanted to pay her under the table, it would be the best thing. She wouldn't have to worry about anybody finding her. She would just be Mary… What was an Amish last name…? Smith. Yes, Smith. That was as ordinary as it got.

Maryanne couldn't hide in an abandoned house forever.

And with some money, she would be able to buy a bus ticket and go west. She'd be able to live her dream and act, but she wasn't as starry-eyed about her possibilities as she had been when she was fifteen.

Before.

Now, she knew things didn't always work out the way they were supposed to. Good people did bad things, and bad people did bad things to good people. Worse, most people didn't care either way.

Jerome pulled off of the road at a strip mall. There was a grocery store, a dollar store, a tax specialist, a nail salon—which Maryanne looked at longingly—and an auto mechanic.

They pulled around the back of the auto shop and parked.

It was loud here. After the first few days of cold and terror in the abandoned farmhouse, Maryanne had gotten used to the quiet. She had grown used to doing the many small tasks she needed to keep herself alive and relatively comfortable, and a sense of adventure had overcome her. She felt bad for stealing, but it was a rush to snatch a dress off one of the drying lines. Or to sneak into a kitchen and take a pot, just a small one, from where it hung from a hook on the wall.

The farmhouse was quiet. No sounds of cars, helicopters or sirens. Not even the hum of the refrigerator or the buzz of a lamp or hum of her laptop. No TV. After she had made her new home as comfortable as she could manage, she thought the quiet would be boring.

And it was, sometimes. But most of the time, Maryanne entertained herself. She wrote in her journal. And sometimes, she tried drawing the pictures in the comics, though she wasn't great at it.

And she walked. There was so much open space here. In her Amish clothing, so long as she stayed near the fields and did not talk to anybody, she blended in. It was fun being invisible. Nobody expected anything of her. She could be herself.

Now, she felt exposed. Everything was loud and strange. The smell of motor oil and exhaust filled her nostrils as they walked to the back entrance.

Jerome asked, "Mary, are you all right?"

Maryanne nodded.

"First time at a garage, I bet. Don't worry, it's loud, but as long as you don't do something stupid like get between Christine and her wrench, you'll be all right."

Maryanne glanced at Luke.

"Christine's the head mechanic," Luke explained.

And then they were inside.

A line of customers stood in front of the desk.

Behind the counter, dressed in a navy jumpsuit with a tool belt hanging from his waist, stood a chubby, light brown man with black, coiled hair, receding at the temples. He looked back at them and shouted, "Jerome, you're late." His eyes widened as he noticed Maryanne. "Luke, is that your sister?"

Maryanne and Luke at the same time protested; Maryanne holding out her hands in front of her,

"No!" while Luke shook his head and said with almost equal horror, "Ne!"

Jerome said, "She wants to apply for the office job."

Maryanne said, "My name is Mary, sir." She did her best to mimic Luke's accent. Luke's eyes widened in surprise, but he didn't comment.

Maryanne smiled.

"Hmm... Can you file?"

Maryanne had, once or twice, put her father's papers into the filing cabinet, so she nodded. "Some," Maryanne added out of a sense of honesty. "I can learn," she added.

Luke said, "Mary is very hard working, Mr. Johnson."

"One day I'll get you to call me Eddie." Mr. Johnson shook his head. "If Luke says you're hard working, Mary, then I'm happy to give you a shot. Come here." He added, "You don't have anywhere else you have to be, do you?"

Maryanne shook her head. It was that easy? She glanced back at Luke. It was that easy with Luke's recommendation. Which she had hardly earned. Maryanne did not want to sully Luke's reputation at his job, so she smiled and, hoping she did not mess things up too badly, walked to Mr. Johnson's side.

He walked her through his system for who had scheduled an appointment, which was both in an antique computer with a large, square monitor, and on carbon sheet paper. Mr. Johnson said, "You have to press down hard with the pen for the customer copy. Got it?"

Maryanne nodded. Hopefully, Mr. Johnson would take her confusion and slowness as being due to her being raised on a farm, as opposed to her having never had a part-time job.

"Have you run one of these before?" Mr. Johnson asked, pointing to the cash register.

Maryanne shook her head. "I'm sorry."

"You're on your rumspringa, right?"

Mary blinked.

"Running around time. That's what you call it, isn't it?"

Mary, not understanding what he was talking about, nodded.

"It's all right. You'll get the hang of this. When Luke got here, he could take an engine apart and put it back together, but he had never seen any of the diagnostics for the newer cars. Now he's a whiz with everything."

While Mr. Johnson was instructing Maryanne, he also consulted with each customer about their car, so by the time they finished the morning rush, Maryanne felt like she had a theoretical knowledge of what she was supposed to be doing.

Mr. Johnson said, "It's quiet from now until after lunch. I'm going to need you to get these into the computer. At the end of the day, you print out a transaction register. I'll show you." He reached behind the computer and pulled out a dusty, three-ring binder and sat it on the desk in front of her. "This'll give you an idea of what the most common questions are. If you don't know, give a shout, and one of us will come up and help you. All we need you to do is get people checked in and have them wait until one of us can look at their car. Think you'll be okay?"

Maryanne was overwhelmed, but she nodded. "Yes, thank you, Mr. Johnson."

"Eddie," he said, clapping her on the back. "And tell Luke he does not have to be so formal, not that he listens. You can leave some… What is it…? English clothes! Yes, you can leave some here to change into, if you want."

Maryanne blinked at him again. English was what Amish people called non-Amish people, wasn't it? She tried to remember back to what Luke had said. Either way, Maryanne was not ready to shed her Amish disguise. She asked, "Do I have to change?"

"Let's see how things work out. We can get you a uniform. Or just a name tag at least." He clapped her on the back again. "Don't look so scared. You'll do fine. Luke vouches for you, so I know you'll do fine."

Maryanne took her place behind the desk. There was a small heater beneath it, pouring hot air over her legs. The door to the garage opened, and a woman came in, leading a child with her right hand. "I'm sorry, I'm late. Overslept," she said. "I have my car for inspection."

Maryanne smiled. In her most cheerful voice, holding on a hint of Luke's Amish accent, she said, "Great! Can I have your name?"

7

Susie had spent much of the previous afternoon making soup, and now she had three large plastic containers in the back of the buggy for Mrs. Fisher. The older woman often had colds, and even when she didn't, she enjoyed both visitors and "sharing news." Not gossip, *news*. Gossip was against the Ordnung. But the sharing of news, so long as they did not speak with ill intent, was fine. As she insisted on multiple occasions.

Mrs. Fisher's "sharing of news" was often informative, if long-winded. Susie doubted they would give her such latitude if her brother wasn't the Bishop. Susie figured the Bishop partook of "sharing of news" himself. At least on the receiving end. How else could he know everything that happened within the confines of their small community?

Besides soup stock and a separate container for vegetables, Susie had brought whoopie pies, "for the children," though Mrs. Fisher snagged desserts before offering sweets to anyone else in her household.

Joseph helped Susie carry the baked goods and soup to Mrs. Fisher's front porch. Susie knocked.

The door opened a crack. "Susie Zook, is that you?" Mrs. Fisher, a squat, middle-aged woman with dark brown hair salted with gray, peered out from the gap with one light-green eye.

"Yes, Mrs. Fisher."

Mrs. Fisher opened it the rest of the way. "Susie Zook and her strapping husband!" Mrs. Fisher's nose was red and chapped from frequent colds. She smiled as her gaze rested on Margaret who clutched a small pan with several plastic-wrapped whoopie pies. "Is that Greta? Are you not just the sweetest thing?"

Margaret stared at Mrs. Fisher and stepped closer to her mother.

Susie said, "It's okay, Margaret." She met Mrs. Fisher's gaze. "Greta is just shy."

"Margaret. Such an English name!" Mrs. Fisher's voice rose, though she had heard Margaret's name hundreds of times in the past four years. "You named her because of your friend Salome, was it?"

Susie nodded. She had told no one besides Joe about the berrying trip and the promise between herself and Salome, merely telling others Salome had favored the English form. Mrs. Fisher had always felt affronted at Susie's evasiveness. Without context, Susie explained, "It was a promise I made to Salome."

Susie had a right to keep her own counsel on some things.

Joe said, "I have to deliver some shelves to Mr. Patterson's store, so I'll pick Susie back up on the way home.

Mrs. Fisher said, "Gutt! I don't want to hold you up, Joseph."

Joseph carried the soup to the kitchen and put it on the counter. Susie did the same with her parcels and Margaret the whoopie pies. When everything was set down, Mrs. Fisher said, "My niece's boy and girl are out working in the barn. Greta, will you take them some pies? And one for yourself?"

Margaret nodded.

Mrs. Fisher took a pair of whoopie pies for herself before handing the rest to Margaret. "Down the stairs, across the way, and go inside. You mind the horses."

Margaret nodded again.

Mrs. Fisher's kitchen had a back door with a set of stairs heading down, and with her gaze Susie traced her daughter's path to the barn.

"Don't you worry, Susie," Mrs. Fisher said. "It's good she does some things on her own. Greta's a quiet child, isn't she?"

"Joe says she just doesn't have so much to say."

Mrs. Fisher tightened her lips. "Little girls always have things to say. Do you talk with her?"

"I do. And I spoke with her pediatrician."

Mrs. Fisher let out a half. "Englishers."

"Dr. Michaels is concerned she isn't hitting her milestones, but she can read a little."

"From the Bible?"

"My friend got her an illustrated one, for children." And a couple of other, less Biblically centric books, but Susie kept that to herself.

Mrs. Fisher, her nose twitching and eyes narrowed like a dog scenting a rat in the barn, asked, "Don't let those Englishers dictate how you should raise your child. If Greta understands her Bible, that's the best. We are not English. Better we concern ourselves with the developmental milestones of the soul."

Susie had no choice but to nod in agreement. She said, "Hannah said you were ill. You look much improved."

Mrs. Fisher nodded. "I am improved." She coughed, a bit dramatically, turning her head away from Susie and pressing a handkerchief to her mouth. "But the cough lingers, some."

Susie said, "Joe and I are both praying for your full recovery."

Mrs. Fisher took the sentiment as her due. She glanced over at the containers of soup Susie had brought. "This will help. It's Gott's blessing I was the only one who truly suffered. I worry for the children. My niece's boy and girl. Especially the girl. She is young and suffers so when she catches a cold. I told her mother to put garlic under the child's pillow. It loosens the phlegm. I hope she listened."

Susie nodded again.

Mrs. Fisher took the whoopie pie she had snagged and turned to the cabinet to pull out a pair of plates. "This looks delicious, my dear. I could not eat the whole thing. But perhaps we could share it? And I'll put the kettle on. Just milk?"

Susie nodded. Mrs. Fisher had a memory like a

steel trap, though she pretended, at points, it was failing. She cut the whoopie pie into four uneven pieces and, taking a pair of saucers, walked them both to the kitchen table.

When the teakettle whistled, Susie poured two cups of hot water over a pair of second use tea bags drying in a small gravy train on the back of the sink.

Susie blew on her tea.

Mrs. Fisher asked, "How is Greta doing, after the church meeting, I mean?"

Susie tensed. Beanpole hadn't hurt Margaret, and in fact, when asked, she had said only that they talked about the chickens. Margaret had asked about chickens, and Beanpole responded. Margaret said they were hungry. Susie shook her head, and said, "Beanpole didn't *do* anything. But I don't like him around her. Or any of the children."

Mrs. Fisher nodded. "With his history…"

Susie blew on her tea again and took a sip. "Hannah told me someone had stolen something from her clothesline. A dress."

Mrs. Fisher took the largest quarter of the whoopie pie and placed it on her plate. She always took the largest piece. "I know I shouldn't be eating this, what with my cholesterol and the medications they have me on, but..."

Susie took a piece and nibbled at it. This freed Mrs. Fisher to take a large bite, which she did, chewing and smiling with an appreciative noise as she swallowed. "Susie Zook, you are a fine, *fine* cook."

Susie smiled.

Mrs. Fisher sipped her tea. "Ja. It is the strangest thing. I asked some of the other ladies, not as gossip, but because we need to know if one of the youths or—Gott forbid—English are stealing from us. My small pot is missing. And someone had rearranged things..." she waved a hand towards a series of hooks her husband had embedded into the wall to the right of the stove. "The pot was hanging right there. I thought that maybe my niece had borrowed it, or one of the kids, you understand...

"But no, it's missing. And five days ago something got the hens riled up. We used to have a rooster, but he died. Poor thing." And Mrs. Fisher had not replaced him. Mrs. Fisher and her husband had both despised that rooster. "I am also missing two pairs of my pressure socks. They are expensive, and I have to get them from the pharmacy.

"Mrs. King said someone took a loaf of bread

off of her stovetop where it was cooling. I've spoken to my brother about it. This isn't gossip, ne," Mrs. Fisher assured Susie, "but be careful of your things. A vagrant must be around, though I've seen no signs. Usually there are cigarettes or some other sign besides thieving. Sometimes they'll come knocking for work and a place to board. The poor man, whoever he is, must be sleeping in the fields I suppose."

"Are you sure it's a vagrant?" Susie asked.

"What else would it be?" Mrs. Fisher asked. She leaned forward in her chair. Whipped cream clung just above her upper lip.

Susie took another bite of her whoopie pie. The whipped cream was too sweet. She washed it down with the tea, still hot enough to burn her tongue. "Would a vagrant steal an Amish girl's dress?"

"We had wondered at first if there wasn't some...perverted man," Mrs. Fisher's eyes widened. "Do you think it is a young woman?"

A woman? Susie hadn't considered it. She bit her lower lip.

"An English woman, sleeping in our fields? Oh my! I must speak with Elijah."

"When did the thefts start?"

"Just before the last church meeting."

Beanpole had returned to the district three weeks ago. If he was responsible, he might have waited for his parents and the community to grow complacent about his presence.

Or maybe, Susie was wrong. Maybe Beanpole had nothing to do with the thefts. Still, the timing... Susie said, "Beanpole returned three weeks before that."

Mrs. Fisher's eyes gleamed. "Do you think Beanpole...stole them? He kept an entire house for Salome... Before and after..." Mrs. Fisher reached out and put her hand on top of Susie's. The Amish weren't so free with their touch, but Mrs. Fisher had always been the sort to hold an acquaintance's hand or lean in with uncomfortable intimacy.

"If it is Beanpole..." Mrs. Fisher shook her head. "I know it is our place to forgive, but stealing is against the Ordnung. And if he is at that house again...! Beanpole makes Hannah uncomfortable, but Jumbo says his son is adjusting and doing well."

Jumbo had ignored all evidence of Beanpole's actions for years. He was hardly a reliable witness with his son.

"That is what Jumbo would say. He loves his family. Emma. Beanpole. Jumbo is a good man, and he faces a hard test with his wife and his son."

Susie grit her teeth. She ought to care for Jumbo's feelings, but what had he done for Salome? What had he done to stop his son from hurting her? How had a good man so turned away from the sins in his own home?

Susie sipped her tea.

"You're still troubled," Mrs. Fisher said. "Don't be. It's just a vagrant. This has happened before. Perhaps it is a young woman instead of a young man. Or an older woman. We do not know. Whoever it is, we will find them, help them if we can, and send them on their way."

"And if it is Beanpole?" Susie's heart sped up. "Would we send him on his way?"

"It may have to be so," Mrs. Fisher said. "My brother was of two minds about allowing him to return. The Millers have family in Indiana, and they could have gone there. But my brother prayed on the situation, as much as he could, and he said he felt Beanpole deserved a second chance." Mrs. Fisher sipped her tea. "But as for a third chance…? No. Beanpole will not have a third. Already, his presence is causing strife within the community. First, his behavior with your daughter at the church meeting, and others are also uncomfortable.

Hannah, and some of the other young ladies. They would rather he leaves."

Susie nodded. She felt reassured knowing others wished Beanpole to leave. Yes, he had repented, but how was it enough?"

Susie asked, "I was hoping I might speak with some of the others who were missing things. Just to have a clear idea of what was happening."

Ms. Fisher laughed. "You want to look into things yourself, isn't it?"

"I do not mean to presume."

"You are the one who found Salome. Presuming a little is in your nature, but does us no harm. You will want to speak with Mrs. Yoder, and the Kings. Also, be careful of your own things and keep a close eye your daughter. She is the only child Beanpole has spoken with since he returned."

Susie shivered. It was no secret Susie had chosen Margaret's name to keep a promise to Salome. Maybe the name had drawn Beanpole's interest. Susie felt cold. She'd wanted to honor her friend, but she would not put her daughter in harm's way. "I will watch her." Susie glanced at the barn.

"There's no way in or out except through the

main doors," Mrs. Fisher said. "I just meant she shouldn't be alone."

Susie took another small bite of her Whoopie Pie.

Mrs. Fisher began her second quarter.

"Now," Mrs. Fisher said after swallowing a second bite. "Let me tell you about Mrs. Yoder's new puppy. Why she chewed through…"

Susie let Mrs. Fisher's "shared news" wash over her as she sipped her tea. She did not know if Beanpole was involved in the thefts, but if incriminating evidence came to light, then the elders would force him and his family to leave.

Susie resolved to keep looking for evidence. The sooner they forced Beanpole out, the better for all.

8

Usually Luke paid close attention to his work, but he was distracted by Marion behind the desk, smiling and chatting with the other customers. He was drawn to her laughter, the way she leaned over the computer, worrying her full lower lip as she typed, the curve of her cheek, and the hint of her form beneath her too lose Amish dress.

Marion was pretty. Beautiful even. But it wasn't just her beauty. It was the way she looked at him as though she found him fascinating and fun. With her, he wasn't boring Luke who organized his tools so they were in size order and polished them until they shined. With her, he was a hero.

In the well between cars, Jerome leaned over

Luke's shoulder as he was reorganizing his space. "You've got it bad," Jerome said.

"Got what?" Luke whispered, though he had a good idea what his friend was referring to. Jerome dug his elbow into Luke's side and glanced at Marion who was smiling and writing something down.

Luke said, "She's great at this, isn't she?"

"So, is Mary new to your district?"

Luke nodded. "She just… Um… Moved a couple of weeks ago." It wasn't a lie, not exactly.

"Well I think she's into you too, so you'd better snap her up before someone else taps that."

"I'm not going to—!"

Jerome laughed and clapped Luke on the shoulder. "I know. I know."

From behind them, Christine, the lead mechanic asked, "Tap what?" Her tone could have frozen a lake.

"Nothing," Jerome mumbled. Luke looked over his shoulder at Christine, a short, stocky woman with close-cut blond curls. Christine was strong. In the summer, she unzipped the uniform and tied the sleeves around her waist, revealing a tank top beneath, her biceps bulged and corded muscle ran down her arms.

"I'm sorry, Christine," Luke said.

Christine had tried, with little success, to get Luke to call her "just Chris," but Luke couldn't bring himself to be disrespectful, so Christine was their best compromise.

Christine said, "Luke, *you* have nothing to apologize for."

Jerome mumbled, "My bad."

Mr. Johnson called out, "Oil change up front!"

"I've got it," Jerome said, and jogged away with more gusto than necessary.

A minute after, Jerome left, Christine asked, "So, do you like Mary?"

Luke swallowed. "I don't know her well."

"That's not what I asked." Christine's voice was low, almost a whisper. Still, Luke's face warmed.

Christine said, "Ask her out."

"I can't!"

"You're supposed to be dating now, aren't you? For your rumspringa?"

"Ja, but I don't know where to take her." Luke looked down at the 1998 Dodge truck he had on his list for an engine check. "Mary has a lot... I don't want to..."

"Invite her to come out with some of your

friends. I know you Amish kids have group activities with your community. Has she taken part?"

"Not yet. She's still settling in."

"She's just hoping somebody will invite her. You should do it. Or take her out to dinner. Eddie will let you borrow the Shelby you've been working on." Christine suggested, "I know you got the engine going. You got your license, didn't you?"

Luke nodded. He rarely drove, even though on his rumspringa he was allowed, but he didn't want to get too comfortable driving. He might like it too much and want to leave. Without him, who would help his mamm with money to keep the house?

At the same time, he loved working on cars, and he'd gotten his driver's license in part for the job and in part for the love of pressing the gas and having the car come to life, rushing towards an uncertain but possibly exciting future as the wind whipped through the open windows.

Would Marion even agree to go?

Marion was hiding in the old Crawley house for a reason. He hadn't mistaken her nervousness or the way she had initially averted her face from the passing cars. She had loosened up today, putting on a bright smile and chatting with everyone who came in for a repair or general maintenance. But meeting strangers at a job is different from socializing. He didn't know how long she planned to stay here. Maybe all she wanted was to earn enough money to run off somewhere else.

Luke couldn't let himself get too attached. She was going to California to be an actress, not staying here to become an Amish wife.

Marion laughed, and Luke couldn't help looking back at her. His heart thumped, and felt a curl of interest, just like when he had kissed Sadie, except stronger. Marion wasn't even looking at him, and yet, Luke felt like he was kissing her. Kissing her would be better than kissing Sadie. He knew it in his bones.

Luke had no business thinking such thoughts about a woman who he would never marry. Still, he thought them.

And worse, a small part of him he desperately wanted to ignore, asked, "What if she stayed?"

"Ask her out," Christine said.

And then there were more cars and more work, and the afternoon sped by. It had been too busy to stop for more than a few minutes at lunch. Marion had stayed at the desk, typing with one hand while absently eating her sandwich with the other.

After closing, Luke asked, "Do you mind if we use your shower?"

Jerome raised both eyebrows. "We're at work, man!"

Luke breathed in sharply, realizing what he implied. "Not that way, I meant, one at a time."

Christine laughed. "Of course, one at a time. Does she have something to change into?"

"She'll be fine," Luke said. Fortunately for him, he had made a habit of showering at the job most days. He got too dirty to subsist with a weekly bath, and bathing daily at home seemed too much of an indulgence, both for the increase in his home water bill, the fuel to power the generator for the hot water heater and the time it took every day to power it up at home. A shower at work was quicker.

Jerome said, "Best be glad I don't have much to do tonight. Your girlfriend's not going to take forever at it, is she?"

"She's not my girlfriend."

"And she won't be if you don't up your game, man."

"My game is fine."

"Alright. Alright."

"I can call for a taxi, if we're holding you up."

Luke should have considered the imposition he was putting on Jerome by having to wait for them.

Jerome laughed. "It's no biggie," he said, wiping his sleeve over his forehead. Me and Kayla were texting anyway. I'm going to see if she wants to see a movie tomorrow night." For all Jerome's trash talking, he was nervous around girls. Especially those he wanted to date. He'd promised to ask Kayla out for weeks. But they were still texting. Luke, living in the same glass house, just nodded. "Good luck," he said.

Christine, shedding her tool belt, said, "I'll walk you back to the shower, Mary."

Luke was relieved he didn't have to take her to the shower and show how the hot and cold spigots were reversed. It was too personal. He knew he didn't have to be "boring, always doing the right thing" Luke on his rumspringa, but he didn't want to ruin whatever chance he might have with Marion by being a jerk either.

Not that he had any chances with her. She would leave as she'd come, a ghost.

When Christine returned, she clapped Luke on the back. "Nice girl. Eddie likes her. So do I. A little shy, but I guess that's expected. I let her use my shower gel. You'd think I gave her a hundred dollars." Christine chuckled. "I dropped a bug in Ed's ear about giving her a little advance so she can get some new boots. They look like they've mucked a dozen stables."

Luke hadn't looked at her shoes. They were tan boots, leather and water stained. The sole had started to come away on the right side. He could see it separate when she walked.

How had Marion ended up at the old Crawley house? They were further west than Philadelphia, but this wasn't the way anyone would pick to go to California. Especially if you needed work. Wouldn't she take an airplane or a train?

Not that it looked like Marion could afford either.

Luke was glad he had helped her. If Marion worked here, they could walk together to Jerome's car early in the morning, and he could walk her back to the house after work.

Maybe he should ask Marion out. She was pretty, nice, interesting, and also a little sad. She'd lost her family, and the English hadn't done much to take care of her afterwards. Why else would she be living in an abandoned house in borrowed clothes and falling-apart boots? He wanted to take that sadness from her. He wished he could invite her to Saturday's youth volleyball game.

None of the others would believe she was Amish though. She did not speak their language, and while she mimicked his accent well, it wasn't the same. Often, at the game, they dropped into Pennsylvania Dutch. She wouldn't understand.

When Marion came out from the back, her hair damp and tied back—not pinned—in a bun, her prayer cap askew atop it, Luke couldn't stop staring. Her skin was flushed, and she grinned.

Luke gave her an awkward nod and dashed to the back to shower himself. A light floral scent hung in the air as Luke stepped into the small, square shower room. The tile was an ugly gray, grayer at the caulk with years of rinsed dirt and oil. Luke had a basic shampoo and body wash, which he used quickly, changing from his uniform to a pair of slacks and a simple shirt. He sprayed the uniform with a clothing refresher and, hanging it on his forearm, left the shower stall to rejoin the others.

Marion and Mr. Johnson were in deep conversation.

The radio, which had been playing classic R&B hits, as usual, faded into a commercial. Luke crossed the room to Marion. "Are you ready?" he asked.

Mr. Johnson looked up at Luke and said, "We will try a two-week probation. Mary says she's fine to come in with you and Jerome from Monday to Saturday. We close at two on Saturdays."

Marion nodded.

Christine, who had just finished putting away her tools, said, "Sounds like that guy was black-mailing a lot of people."

"What guy?" Luke asked.

"The one who was shot…Timothy something or other. It was all over the news last week. He was an aide to Robert Baldwin, the police captain who's running for mayor."

Marion paled and looked down. Her hands shook.

Luke averted his gaze, his mind humming. Why did this guy's death scare her so much? Maybe she had a more sinister reason for hiding in the old Crawley house?

No, he couldn't believe she'd do something bad. Not really bad.

"Lots of people wanted Tim dead, it seems. There's a witness, or maybe she did it, they don't know. Someone saw her in Lancaster."

"A woman?"

Christine shrugged. "Women are just as capable as men."

"Just because she was there doesn't mean she killed anyone," Marion cut in.

"Then why'd she run?"

"Maybe she was scared."

"She'd better come up and say what she saw then. There's a reward. Five-thousand dollars. It's not a lot, but..."

"Who's offering a reward?" Jerome asked.

"You think you're going to cash in?" Christine shook her head. "That girl is far from here by now. Lancaster's not Philly, but it's a big enough city to catch a ride out.

"She'd be stupid to stick around," Marion said, looking down at her hands. "How do they know what she looks like?"

"Camera. It only got the side of her head though as she ran out. I bet they tracked her phone too, but..." Christine shook her head. "Doesn't matter. That Timothy had his fingers in a lot of pies."

Marion bit her lower lip. "You think he deserved it?"

"No one deserves it. Sometimes though, people

bring things on themselves. Keep your head down, mind your own business, that's what I say."

"Yeah...ja..."

"You're sheltered. It works like this with the English, sometimes."

"Mary!" Mr. Johnson stood by the register, beckoning Marion to come over.

Marion said, "Excuse me," and left.

Luke followed. Did she have something to do with Timothy, something or other's death? Marion was not a murderer. Whatever had happened, it wasn't Marion's fault. Luke didn't know why he was so sure of this, but he was.

Mr. Johnson reached into the register, took four twenty-dollar bills and handed them to Marion. "Don't worry about that girl. They'll find her." He looked up. "God willing."

"I've only worked one day," Maryanne said.

"You don't want the job?"

"I do!" Marion said.

"Good." Mr. Johnson looked down at her shoes. "We'll call today a paid trial. See if you can't get a pair of work boots for next week. I don't know if you'll have time to pick up new ones before tomorrow, but this weekend...?"

Marion blushed. "I'm sorry," she said.

"I just don't want to see them ruined."

"Thank you."

Jerome dropped them off at the side of the road where he had picked them up this morning. He said, "Tomorrow, seven AM?"

Marion nodded.

Jerome added, "And, hey.... If the two of you are free Saturday night...?"

Marion cocked her head. "Yes?"

"I know you and Mary aren't dating, but if you want to come with me and Kayla to see a movie, it could be fun."

Luke grinned. "You asked her!"

Jerome averted his gaze, looking at his hands on the wheel. "Yeah. It's not anything. She wants to see the new Marvel movie, and, I know you like comics, and—whatever."

Luke glanced at Marion. "We can see movies on our rumspringa."

She asked, "Do you want to see it?"

"I wouldn't want to be a third wheel."

Marion said, "We don't have to wear... *English* clothes...?"

"No. You know that." Marion probably didn't, and Luke claiming she did was close to a lie, but it was his rumspringa too. He had not taken his

Kneeling Vows yet, and besides, the whole ruse was a lie.

Marion nodded. "I want to."

Luke grinned. The expression hurt his cheeks. Lying was a sin, and he would have to repent for it, but it thrilled him Marion wanted to go out with him. Maybe she only wanted to see the movie, but it hardly mattered.

They finished saying their goodbyes and Jerome drove off.

Marion said, "I guess I should go back to the house now."

They had stopped at a drive-through on their way back, and Marion carried the remains of her dinner and a pair of breakfast sandwiches in a paper bag in her left hand.

Luke said, "I can put your food in our refrigerator for you, and bring it back tomorrow."

"Denki," Marion said.

"That sounded right," Luke said. "You are great with the accent."

Marion shrugged. "I've always been good with accents.

The air was chilly, and as they walked together along the roadside, wind gusted over their faces. Marion wore a dark gray peacoat with large, black buttons. It differed from what the Amish girls in Luke's district would wear. It hugged her frame, accentuating the silhouette of her curves. Luke's mouth felt dry. His palms sweated. He wiped them on his much duller Navy jacket.

Luke ventured. "What happened to you?" He wouldn't ask about the dead guy. Marion was scared enough without Luke accusing her of something. "I just want to help."

Maybe the killer was after her?

It was too much like a comic book. Maybe he'd read too many of them, too young. He'd broken the rules to do it and now he imagined himself a hero.

"I know," Marion said. The strings of her prayer cap had come loose, and she worried at one, further tilting the cap on her head. "You are helping."

A tuft of wavy hair, forced free of its ragged bun, swept down from her temple. Luke wanted to tuck it behind her ear, but that would be too forward.

"You are helping so much." Marion's voice cracked. "I can't even tell you how much."

Resolve simmered in Luke. He lifted his chin against whatever obstacles they might face. "Whoever you're running from, I will not let them hurt you."

"I'm fine," Marion said, bowing her head. Was she crying?

Luke took her hand, giving her enough time to pull away if she wanted. But her grip tightened around his hand.

They walked together hand-in-hand to the house.

At the base of her stairs, Luke said, "I'll see you tomorrow then."

Luke should have let go of Marion's hand at that point. He was tired and sore and there were still chores at home to do. If he was too late, his mother would worry about him. He was already later than usual stopping to walk Marion home.

Not home. Just the place she was staying. For now.

Marion said, "I'm sorry. For everything."

"Don't go."

"What?"

"Just be here tomorrow. Please. And if anything happens, and you need a place to stay..." he gave her his address and had her repeat it.

Marion nodded. "I'll be okay. I promise. I didn't do anything. I swear."

"I believe you."

Marion swallowed. "You do?"

"You're a good person."

"I'm not."

"Whatever happened, I think you are very brave," Luke said.

Marion's shoulders shook. She lifted her free hand to wipe her sleeve under her eye. Her cheeks were damp.

"Don't cry," Luke said, helplessly.

"I'm not brave," Marion said.

Luke pulled her to him. She lifted her chin, and they were kissing. The salt of her tears mingled with the sweetness of her lips, and Luke was lost.

Marion stepped back, pulling her hand away. "Tomorrow," she said.

The ground beneath Luke's feet shook. Or maybe it was just his legs were weak. "I'm sorry," he said, though he wasn't unless his kiss had been unwelcome.

"Don't be. Never."

"You are so beautiful," Luke said in Pennsylvania Dutch.

"What does that mean?" Marion asked.

Luke's face was hot. "Until tomorrow," he lied.

Marion repeated the words back to him, syllable

by syllable, as though she was practicing a song. It was near note perfect. Luke's face, already hot, now felt like it was on fire. "Denki," he mumbled.

Luke hadn't much experience with kissing. There was only Katie by the creek behind the school when he was twelve, and Sadie. Neither kiss had felt like this. The memory lingered as he said his goodbyes and lingered like the fading heat of an embrace as he walked home.

9

The stolen goods ate at Susie as she drove the buggy to the grocery store in town. Margaret sat behind her, humming to herself as she played with a cloth doll.

Susie preferred to shop for groceries in the morning, but Joseph had needed the buggy to take two chairs he had made to one of the local shops. The driver was ill, and the distance was short enough the journey would not overtax their horse.

Joe returned after lunch with a bag of sugar-free hard candies for Margaret. The little girl took them and, grinning, threw herself into her father's arms.

While the Amish were not affectionate in public, in the comfort of their own home, Joseph showered his wife and daughter with signs of his love. Small gifts. Ruffling his daughter's hair, tossing her into the air, and embracing the pair of them.

Margaret occupied herself with the candies while Joe gave his wife a slow kiss. "As their lips parted, he murmured, "Wife, I love you."

Susie swallowed. "I love you too, Joe. More than I can ever say." In Joseph's arms, the fear she was failing him faded. In his arms, she felt like she could manage anything. But then he stepped back, and said, "We have a new commission. A young couple bought the chairs, and they want another pair for their kitchen table. You take the buggy, and I'll get started on it this afternoon.

Susie nodded. Joe did not need to explain why he was so industrious. He had been saving all extra funds for their family fund, expecting at the least another few siblings for Margaret.

The crushing sense of failure was back. Joseph always claimed the additional time to save was a blessing, and that Gott would deliver more blessings in his own time. After almost three years, Susie's faith in Gott stayed strong, but she doubted herself.

Dear Gott, she prayed, *I know you cannot demand of you more than is your will, but if it is I who is failing, please, show me what I must do.*

Joe rested two fingers beneath Susie's chin. "Susie, are you okay?"

"Ja." She nodded again. "Just thinking of everything we need to get. Was there anything you wanted?" Aside from the gingersnap snacks and salted peanuts he always wanted. "Beyond your usual?"

"Whatever you decide is always wonderful, Susie."

Susie was so blessed already. She could not ask for a better husband nor did she want one. She smiled, and he kissed her again.

But the sense she was failing haunted her as she led Margaret to the buggy. She had failed Salome. She was failing Joe. And then there was the matter of the thief.

The tally of stolen items included: a hairbrush, a half a roll of toothpaste, three pairs of socks, a loaf of bread, an apron, the small pot Mrs. Fisher lamented, a medium-sized frying pan, and some canned goods, though none except Mrs. Fisher were quite so organized as to remember what or when the canned goods might have gone missing.

None of the items, of themselves, were troubling. The thefts spoke to, as Mrs. Fisher had surmised, a vagrant in the area. One who, aside from his, or perhaps her, assortment of thefts, had caused no other obvious trouble.

It was even possible the person had moved on, as the thefts had stopped over a week ago. And yet, Susie could not let go. These stolen items could be used to play house for another victim.

Beanpole claimed he had killed Salome attempting to defend her from an English attacker, but he'd filled the old Crawley house with goods for a married couple. Beanpole could have kidnapped and "tended house" with Salome until she tried to escape. He might even believe his own story of trying to defend her, but that did not make it true. Now, within a month of Beanpole's return to the community, small items suitable for a young woman were going missing.

Someone needed to follow Beanpole and make sure he wasn't getting away from his parents to steal from the others in the community.

But how could Susie follow him? Even if she didn't have to care for Margaret, she had no reason to shadow Beanpole.

It was past three when Susie pulled the buggy up and parked in the line of horses and buggies. After tying her horse, she, Margaret at her side, walked to the entrance and took a shopping cart.

It was a large, English superstore with bright lights and an abundance of blowing heat. Pushing the cart, Susie crossed the threshold, and, list in hand, started down the produce aisle.

Margaret gripped Susie's skirts as they walked. Remembering what the English doctor had explained to her about encouraging Margaret to use verbal communication, Susie pointed towards the produce and asked, "Those oranges look good, don't they?"

Margaret nodded.

Right. Susie had to ask open-ended questions. Susie tried again. "Which do you like better, the big ones or the little ones?"

Margaret pointed at the boxes of clementines.

Susie pushed the cart closer. "What oranges are those?"

"Little."

It was then, looking over the oranges towards the fresh spinach, glistening beneath occasional sprays of water from above, Susie saw Beanpole.

Beanpole pushed a cart between his mother, who leaned forward, looking over the cabbages, and his father, who stood, expression unblinking, arms folded, staring off down the aisle.

Beanpole slouched, leaning his weight on the

cart, tapping at the bar of the shopping cart with his index finger. He sighed and rubbed his knuckles on his cheek. His sleeve dropped revealing a splash of bright red around his wrist.

A ribbon.

A red ribbon.

Susie's guts turned to ice. The air was damp, heavy with the smell of mingled greens with a hint of strawberry. Nothing sinister about it, but Susie's hands shook.

She looked at Beanpole again, but he had taken hold of the cart again, and his sleeve hid the offending ribbon.

Margaret tugged on Susie's skirt. Susie forced a smile, gripping tight on the box of clementines as she leaned to her daughter. "Yes, sweetie?"

Margaret pointed at Beanpole. Susie dropped the box of clementines and grabbed her daughter's hand, pulling it down. "Ne!" Her heart pounded.

Margaret stared. "Mamm?" Her lower lip trembled.

"Come," Susie said. "We have enough produce." They didn't. Susie's list called for broccoli, cauliflower and cabbage, but Susie could not stay here. Not with Beanpole hiding a red ribbon on his wrist. The missing items, the hidden ribbon, sent

Susie back to five years ago when she had seen him in the store purchasing red ribbon for Salome's hidden grave.

Salome had promised, "When I am on my rumspringa, I will wear red ribbons in my hair every day."

Susie's throat ached. Hate coiled from her chest to her belly in a loop of tightening agony. She turned the shopping cart around, keeping a sharp eye on Margaret. "It's okay, Greta," Susie reassured her daughter. "Everything is going to be okay."

"Susie!" Hannah called out from Susie's right, beside the specialty cheeses.

Susie, relieved to see a friendly face, smiled at Hannah. Pushing the cart, she closed the distance between them. "I'm finished here," Susie said, averting her body from where Beanpole and his family were shopping. "Can we go?" She waved further into the store.

"Ja."

They were in the canned goods aisle before Hannah spoke. "Beanpole and his parents often shop at this time of day."

"You've been following him?" Susie asked.

"Are you going to report me to the elders?"

Susie shook her head. "I'm grateful."

Hannah smiled, taking three cans of diced tomatoes from the shelf and putting them into her shopping cart. She glanced over at Susie's. "Your clementines… Some of them fell." Without waiting for Susie to rearrange them, Hannah leaned over and fished out a pair, tossing them back into the cardboard crate with the others.

Susie asked, "Do you know where Beanpole got the red ribbon?"

Hannah breathed in through her teeth. "What ribbon?"

A stab of irritation passed through Susie; she stepped on it. She couldn't fault Hannah's initiative, even if her observation was lacking. Susie said, "He has a red ribbon tied around his right wrist."

Margaret, who had wandered across the aisle, came back, hugging two cans of peaches. She tapped Susie on the leg. Susie smiled down at her child, who held the cans out. "Please?" She asked in Pennsylvania Dutch.

"Ja," Susie agreed, holding out her hands. Margaret handed the cans to Susie who put them in the cart. With Beanpole so close, even if under the supervision of his parents, Susie added, "Stay in this aisle, and do not speak with anyone here, do you understand?"

Margaret nodded.

"Gutt," Susie said. Softening her tone, she asked, "Can you get one more can of peaches and a can of fruit cocktail?"

"Ja, Mamm." Margaret rocked back and forth on her feet.

"Wunderbaar!"

Margaret had turned and jogged back towards the peaches.

Susie whispered to Hannah, "Whatever the elders say about Beanpole's change of heart, I do not trust him."

Hannah nodded. "I thought so."

"But I cannot follow him," Susie said. "I have Margaret now and Beanpole would notice me. After what happened with Salome, he'd notice me."

Hannah patted the top of Susie's hand, a light but intimate touch, as though they were close friends. Which, considering their shared suspicions, perhaps they were becoming. Susie asked, "Have you seen anything that might connect him with the stolen items?"

Hannah shook her head. "I can only run into him so many times myself. Katie is also helping. But again, it is difficult."

Susie nodded. Her eyes stung, not with sadness but with relief.

"We'll see something, soon enough. He slipped up before, and he'll slip up again."

Susie closed her eyes. Beanpole would be more cautious now. Before, none has suspected him. Now, all knew of his crime and his repentance.

Susie said, "He is a danger to us."

They only had Beanpole's word he attempted to protect Salome. Though Susie wanted to trust the elders' judgment, Beanpole's word was not enough for her. Knowing that others shared her concerns made Susie feel, for once, she was not alone.

But she could not count on the two women to find the evidence without help.

Susie recognized the plan that was forming in her mind was against the Ordnung. Lying was a sin. But to stop Beanpole, lying would be necessary.

She would do it to ensure Beanpole was cast out of their community. Though she could not involve the other young ladies in the specifics of her plan, she would use them. Susie owed it to Salome to stop Beanpole before he hurt somebody else.

10

_T_he afternoon of Saturday's youth volleyball game was gray and dripping. They set up a net in the Stoltzfus' family barn. The girls wore t-shirts and baggy exercise pants which showed their figures better than the plain dresses for the Sings.

Luke also wore a pair of loose, sweat capris and a tank top. Sadie, Luke's ex, gave him a smile and a wave from across the court.

Luke nodded, surprised at her attention. Since she had begun courting with a young man from a neighboring district, Mark, she had ignored Luke.

Luke glanced around the room for Mark, who was absent. Maybe that's why Sadie had deigned to acknowledge him.

Luke caught his friend Melvin's gaze and, after waving, jogged across court to talk with him.

Melvin was half a head shorter than Luke and stocky with dark brown hair and glasses, black and thick framed, covering his light brown eyes. He said, in a low voice, "Sadie and Mark broke up, did you hear?"

Luke shook his head.

"They had a massive blowout at an English restaurant. That's all I know."

Luke nodded. He glanced back at Sadie. A few months back, her blonde waves and green eyes had filled his dreams. They had talked, and held hands, and even kissed once or twice. He'd imagined himself in love. More than that, he'd imagined she loved him. Now, his memories of her had faded. Nothing could replace the intense moment of connection he had felt with his lips touched Marion's.

Or maybe it was the fact Marion trusted him. And Luke, knowing the value of that trust, gave his to her in turn.

Sadie's gaze rested on Luke, and she smiled, a slow, calculated movement of her lips. Had she always smiled like that?

Luke averted his gaze.

Melvin said, "Sadie wants you back."

"Ne."

Melvin clapped Luke on the shoulder. "Good for you. There are other pretty girls. Has anyone else caught your eye?"

Luke bit the inside of his cheek just enough to feel the pressure. He couldn't talk about Marion. Instead, he shrugged, averting his gaze to the volley-ball net where some of the other guys had gathered to talk.

Melvin leaned in to whisper in Luke's ear. "Who is she?"

Thanks to Gott their coach, Boaz Hoschtetler, called the young men and women over to the net. They were split into teams, a mix of girls and boys. Luke and Sadie were put on the same team. Because two districts of youths were put together for the game, the teams had to rotate players in and out with each serve.

Luke started out on the court, in the middle row. Sadie was beside him, at his right, which meant they would spend some time together on the benches when they were rotated out.

Two months ago, knowing Sadie was single again, Luke would've seized on the opportunity to talk with her and ask her out. From the glances she was casting him, she would be open to the suggestion.

Now, all he wanted was to escape. Luke focused on the game, participating in a pair of volleys that had the other teens cheering and egging on both him and Samuel, a sixteen-year-old boy on the other side of the net.

Too quickly, Luke finished his rotation and, wiping a sleeve on his sweaty forehead, went to the table for a cool glass of water and a handful of cookies.

"Luke!" Sadie called out, making it impossible for Luke to pretend to ignore her.

Luke looked back. "Ja?"

Sadie and another girl, Fanny, walked towards them. Sadie asked, "Luke, how have you been?"

"Fine," Luke said. He took a gulp of his water.

"I hear you're fixing up another one of those classic cars for your employer. How's the restoration going?"

Luke had confessed to Sadie his interest in restoring classic cars, and the project he was working on, 1968 Volkswagen bug. He couldn't help warming to the topic a little. "I just got the seats in, and the engine is running like a dream."

Sadie smiled, soft and slow. "Wunderbar! Mark and I broke up."

"I'm sorry to hear that."

Sadie shrugged. "He wasn't the right guy for me." She wore her prayer cap, but she had pulled her hair up in a loose ponytail with wisps framing her face. It was pretty. Her lips were full and pink. Luke caught a hint of a strawberry scent. She was wearing the lip-gloss she favored. It tasted of strawberries too.

Luke nodded again. "Better to figure it out before you announce an engagement," he said. He grabbed another cookie and started to say his good-byes, but Sadie called out, "Wait!"

Luke cocked his head.

"Sometimes, you do not appreciate what you have until it's gone. Do you understand?"

Sadie had left him. She had been all shining eyes, trembling lips and soft regrets, but ultimately, she had declared him too dull to date, let alone marry.

Though Luke and Marion had no future together, Luke was grateful to Marion for opening his eyes. Marion was squatting in an abandoned house and living a lie. But at least she didn't accuse Luke of being boring.

Oddly, where it counted, Marion was honest.

Maybe because she was so open about her present. Maybe because they both shared a secret instead of her keeping one from him. Or maybe Luke was fickle.

Sadie said, "Fannie and her boyfriend are seeing a movie tonight. We could go with them and make it a double date."

"Ne." Luke wasn't standing Marion up to see a movie with a girl who had dumped him. "I already have a date. Sorry."

"You have a date! With who?"

Sadie's voice was sharp. Her smile had gone hard along with her eyes. "When did you meet?"

"Not long ago," Luke prevaricated. "And you don't know her."

"Well!" Sadie crossed her arms over her chest. "Well… That's gutt for you, I guess."

"Very gutt," Luke said. He was smiling too, hard enough his cheeks ached. He popped the cookie into his mouth, chewed and swallowed. "Have fun," he said. Luke looked towards the volleyball court "I think you're next."

Mr. Hoschtetler was waving them both over. Sadie turned on her heels and, back straight and shoulders stiff, strode over to the court."

Luke finished up his glass of water and strode to the court to take his turn again. Sadie was playing hard, spiking the ball over the net with enough force that the young woman on the opposite side leaped back, hands flailing.

"Sadie!" Mr. Hoschtetler called out. "Bit less force. Good effort though."

Mr. Hoschtetler added, leaning in to Luke who was next to be rotated into the game, "What did you say to her? I've never seen her play this hard."

Luke shrugged.

The coach's lips quirked. "Ah. I should've known."

Luke went in next, and he played though to serving again when the doors of the barn opened and a uniformed English police officer strode in, followed by a brown woman with her hair pulled back in a bun, gray pantsuit with a plain blouse buttoned up to her collar. The woman's gaze flitted over the group.

Mr. Hoschtetler waved to the pair. Luke froze, ball in hand, just swung back to serve. "Mr. Hoschtetler?"

"Keep playing," the coach said. "I'll see what they want."

Luke lined up his serve, and the ball arced over

the net. A short volley followed with Luke's team store scoring a point. They all cheered. In two more points, it would be game.

Luke served again, and the ball flew. The next point went to the other team, and Luke rotated out.

Mr. Hoschtetler called out to halt the game. He waved them all over to the two guests, one of whom held out a police badge.

The English rarely involved themselves in Amish affairs, unless something happened that was so drastic the elders had to call in the English authorities. Like when Susie had found Salome's body buried beneath the oak at the old Crawley house.

Luke recognized neither the officer nor the woman. But he wasn't the type to have the police called on him, like sometimes happened when one the wilder teens got into trouble during their running around time.

Luke joined the others, standing in a half circle around the pair and Mr. Hoschtetler.

Mr. Hoschtetler said, "This is Officer Michaelson," he nodded to the man, "and Detective Gunter with the Philadelphia police department."

Philadelphia police! What were they doing in

Amish country? Luke's mind immediately went to Marion. They'd tracked her here?

The woman said, "I am investigating the murder of Mr. Timothy Eldridge."

Mr. Hochstetler said, "I don't see what that would have to do with us."

"We are looking for this young woman." Detective Gunter pulled a piece of computer paper from her suit jacket. Printed on it was the grainy image of a teen girl in a heavy winter coat, hat and gloves.

Was that Marion?

Maybe. She was the right build, and something in her profile seemed familiar, but he couldn't be sure.

"We believe this woman may have witnessed or been involved in a homicide. If you see her, please call."

"I can't see anything from that picture," Luke blurted out.

The officer said, "I understand, but you Amish folks are known for your close communities here. Also, there have been reports of robberies in the area. We are concerned about this young woman and the safety of your community."

"It is unlikely Miss Buckley is holed up here," Mr. Hoschtetler said with a smile. "But if we see anything unusual, we'll let you know. We prefer to stay out of English affairs, as you know."

Detective Gunter said, reaching into her suit jacket pocket again. "Here's my card. If you do see something," she said, handing a card to Mr. Hochstetler. Her gaze swept over the group. "Call us at this number. That goes for all of you. Who here has a phone?"

A smattering of hands raised. Mr. Hoschtetler said, "If they need to make a call, they know where to go, Detective Gunter."

The detective nodded and waved a hand to the officer, who handed business cards to the rest of the group.

Luke cradled the business card in his palm. His exercise pants did not have pockets, but he would slip it into his bag for later.

Not that he'd need it. Marion had nothing to do with a homicide.

After the detectives had left, the room erupted in conversation.

Sadie's best friend Fannie pulled at her T-shirt. "Do you really think there's a murderer here? I mean, besides Beanpole?"

"Beanpole killed Salome by accident."

"That's what they say."

"We do not gossip!" Mr. Hoschstetler shouted over the group of teens. In the silence that followed, he added, "The English are being cautious, informing everyone in our area in case we see something. It is our duty to cooperate. If we come across this young woman or any suspicious behavior, we must call the English police at once."

Everyone nodded.

Luke felt horrible, keeping Marion a secret. She was hiding in the Crawley house from something or someone. Was it really the police? If she had hurt no one, why didn't she just come forward and confess?

Whatever had happened to Marion, Luke had already vowed to help her. And he would. Luke always did the right thing. He just wasn't sure, right now, what the right thing was. He wanted Marion to stay. How could he trust his own judgment, considering how he was falling for her?

Eventually, Mr. Hoschtetler called them back to the game. Luke played without thinking. He would see Marion tonight. He had chosen his outfit to impress her: a pair of English-style jeans and an off-black button-down shirt were laid out for the evening.

Luke would have to tell her about the police

detective. If Maryanne came forward and cleared the record, they could keep in touch. Luke's neighbor had a phone his barn, and as Luke was still in his rumspringa. He could purchase an English cellphone. He would, if it meant he could speak with Marion again.

$\mathcal{T}$o properly frame Beanpole for the crime of stealing, Susie needed to become a thief herself.

Susie felt ill at the thought. What kind of example was she giving her daughter, robbing their neighbors?

But it had to be done.

Beanpole was a menace. Susie planned Saturday afternoon for her approach. It surprised Joe to see her up so early, baking, but he'd tolerated it, especially when she showed him the whoopie pies she was making for dessert that evening.

By virtue of multiple egg timers, Susie had six loaves of bread and two dozen whoopie pies going along with the breads she wanted to bake for the family.

Joe asked, as Susie was packing the cooled loaves away in tinfoil and putting them into cloth bags to deliver, "Why all at once?"

Susie said, "We don't have church tomorrow, and I want to do a kindness. *Bear ye one another's burdens, and so fulfill the law of Christ.* Hannah is nervous. Mrs. Fisher is having one of her coughs again, and Mrs. Stoltzfus has been so kind to us, opening her barn not only for the church service but also for the youth volleyball team."

Joseph took Susie's hands and pulled her close. "Wife, you are a marvel."

Susie forced a smile as she gazed into her husband's eyes. She was anything but marvelous, and it pained her to see the trust and admiration in her husband's gaze. Beanpole was a menace, and he needed to be cast out of the community, but Susie's methods were not honorable. Nor honest. She was breaking the Ordnung and risking her own family's place to have Beanpole cast out.

"I hope you do not mind walking to your father's today."

A part of her hoped her husband minded.

Hoped he needed the buggy and made it thus impossible to carry out her plan.

"Ne, Susie," Joseph said. He pulled her into a tight embrace. Against her ear, he said, "I will enjoy my walk. The rain refreshes the fields and my heart, almost as much as your love."

Susie squeezed him tighter, breathing in his scent of sawed wood and soap. Her stomach churned. Maybe there was another way. But no other thoughts came to her as Susie finished packing her breads and prepared Star to pull the buggy.

They visited Mrs. Stoltzfus first. Her house was the closest, and she was least likely to notice a missing item before the day, or perhaps a few days, had passed. With so many daughters and sons, Mrs. Stoltzfus had a lot to manage.

Susie gave Margaret the cloth bag with the first loaf of bread and sent her running to the house. Margaret dashed across the driveway and up the stairs to the porch. She balled up her fist and banged on the door. Susie followed. Two of Mrs. Stoltzfus's daughters stood outside on the porch, beating carpeting with large sticks, shaking clouds of dust onto the ground. The finished rugs hung over the porch railing. Maybe Susie could grab one of those?

Ne, too unwieldy.

Margaret waved shyly at the girls, who said, "Greta! Susie!" Mrs. Stoltzfus's oldest daughter added, "Door's open. Mamm will be so glad for your visit, Susie."

"Denki." Susie pushed at the door, which swung easily inwards. "Mrs. Stoltzfus?"

"Who's there?" Mrs. Stoltzfus called out from the back of the house.

"Susie Zook. And Greta Zook."

"What a pleasure! Come on back." They walked together to the kitchen. Standing at the counter, Mrs. Stoltzfus said, "What are you doing out and about? It's going to rain."

"Mamm said rain," Margaret interjected in a rare full sentence.

Mrs. Stoltzfus raised an eyebrow. "Exactly. And my once broken toe agrees." She pointed at the cloth bag Greta had over her shoulder. "What's that, dear?"

Margaret held the bag out. "Bread."

Susie said, "I had made some extra bread on Sunday, and I thought I might deliver some, as you have been so kind, allowing us to have church meeting here two weeks in a row and hosting the youth volleyball sessions.

"That is so lovely! Denki!"

Susie said, "And Greta helped with the packaging and gathering the eggs."

"Of course she did." Mrs. Stoltzfus leaned down, so she was eye to eye with Margaret. "Denki."

Margaret's face colored, and she mumbled, "Welcome."

Mrs. Stoltzfus said, "Why don't we put these on the counter?"

As Susie and Margaret handed the woman the packages, and she placed Susie's loaf of bread on the counter, Susie's gaze caught on a square of cross-stitch hanging beside one of the open windows. The stitches were faded, and the fabric yellowed with age. It read, "A warm heart makes a warm home."

Susie averted her gaze. Mrs. Stoltzfus would certainly miss it and recognize it should the bit of cross-stitch be found again in Beanpole's possession. Susie's stomach roiled. She swallowed, tasting acid in the back of her throat. It was one thing to imagine stealing something inconsequential, and another to contemplate the method of it.

Mrs. Stoltzfus said, "Oh Susie, are you feeling well?" She pulled a stool from the counter where she had been resting while she cooked. "Can you sit here? You haven't caught ill, have you? Or perhaps…?" Mrs. Stoltzfus his eyes shone, and Susie felt even worse about what she had been planning.

Susie shook her head.

"Oh!" After a moment, Mrs. Stoltzfus smiled sadly. "In its own time, Susie," she said. "If it is Gott's will, it will happen in its own time."

Margaret asked, "What time, Mamm?"

Susie wanted her daughter to speak more, and today, Margaret had asked a full question in a full sentence! And yet, Susie could not celebrate. Her heart was too heavy. She swallowed. And said, "Gott's time, Greta. All things in Gott's time."

Margaret looked confused, but thankfully Mrs. Stoltzfus handed the girl a glass of orange juice, which she took, and leaning with her back against the counter, began to drink.

"Gott has truly blessed you, Susie," Mrs. Stoltzfus said, gesturing towards Margaret. "She is a lovely child."

Susie nodded. Margaret was a lovely child. She

said, "We are hoping she can have a little brother or sister soon."

"I know." Mrs. Stoltzfus shook her head. "Have you tried putting a horseshoe under your bed? It is a little superstition, but my mamm swore by it. She would only put the horseshoe when she was ready to have another child, you understand. And not a moment before."

"It worked?"

"It is what she said."

Outside, one of the girls started shouting.

Mrs. Stoltzfus leapt to her feet. "Stay here. I think the rooster got out again." With that, she grabbed a broom by the back door and dashed out the kitchen entrance.

Susie looked over at the cross stitch again.

Margaret followed her gaze. "Pretty," she said.

"It is, isn't it?" Susie said. "Can you put that bottle of orange juice back in the refrigerator?"

Greta nodded.

Before Susie could change her mind, she grabbed the cross-stitch and dropped it into her bag.

After some shouting outside, "You get away from that line!" Mrs. Stoltzfus returned. Her skirts were dusty, and broom straw clung to the hem.

Margaret knelt and pulled a straw free. She handed up to Mrs. Stoltzfus, who smiled and thanked her.

Mrs. Stoltzfus said, "I had best keep an eye on them."

Susie said, "We can see ourselves out. I hope you enjoy the bread."

As Susie settled Margaret into the buggy, the child reached for the bag with the stolen cross-stitch.

"Ne!" Susie shouted.

Margaret dropped the bag, her eyes welling up with tears. "Mamm?"

Susie hated this. She hated scolding Margaret for something that wasn't the child's fault. Susie said, "That bag is special. You can use the next one, after we have visited the Fishers, okay?"

Margaret nodded.

"You leave that bag alone, do you understand?"

Margaret, eyes wide, nodded.

Susie visited three more neighbors, stealing one other item, and left Margaret with Hannah before delivering the final loaf of bread to the Millers.

12

*C*rossing the threshold of the Miller's Farm made Susie shiver. It was late afternoon, and Susie hoped Jumbo and Beanpole were out. Beanpole never had kept up steady work, aside from his job of maintaining the old Crawley house. Jumbo, Beanpole's father, had done a variety of jobs including construction and working part-time stocking shelves at a local store in town. Hopefully, he had arranged for Beanpole to go with him.

She hoped she could get away long enough to plant the stolen items in Beanpole's room. If not, she would put them somewhere in the house and hope for the best.

Besides the two items Susie had taken from the other women, she had added one of her own under dresses. It was large, from when she had been pregnant.

The sky's threatening rainfall came as a chill mist that blurred the driver's window of Susie's buggy and made the buggy's wheels sink into the dirt. What struck Susie most about the farm was how ordinary looked. There were fields, a barn, and a chicken coop with three fat and fluffy hens picking up the dirt in front of it.

Emma stood at the clothesline, pulling sheets down and shaking them. She ambled with no panic or annoyance at the fact her clothing was once again getting wet.

Susie remembered Emma's temper from before and wondered at how much she had changed. It was the therapy, medications, or both.

Perhaps they had changed Beanpole as well?

Maybe. But there was still the red ribbon around his wrist. Whatever changes the medications had made, they had not altered what made him dangerous.

Susie stopped her buggy in front of the house and, leaving the final loaf inside, tied Star to a post and then rushed to help Emma bring in the remains of her laundry.

Emma's eyes widened, and she froze, taking one clothespin from an apron which flapped in the mist.

Susie shouted, "It's me, Susie Zook!"

"Susie Zook?" Emma spoke slowly. "You are Joseph Zook's new wife?"

Not so new. They had been married for over seven years. But Susie nodded and forced a smile. "You look like you need some help."

"It started raining."

Susie nodded. She went to the next dress and pulled it down. "Where do you want this?"

Emma pointed towards the back of her house, where a flight of steps led up to the kitchen entrance. The inside door was open, and the screen rattled in the growing breeze. Susie took two more dresses and a pair of trousers off of the line, dropping the clothespins into the pocket of her apron and hanging the clothing over her arm. In the same time, Emma removed the apron and a second pair of trousers.

"How are you feeling?" Susie asked.

Emma shrugged.

"Your husband? He's out?"

"Him and Beanpole. Got work with a crew building houses. You were friends with Salome. Salome Beiler?" Emma's lips tightened, just for a second, and then she looked back towards the line, grabbing an abandoned clothespin and shoving it into her bag.

Susie nodded. It was odd; she had never spoken to Emma about Salome. Or maybe it was not so odd. The Millers kept to themselves. Jumbo had apologized, after, claiming he had not known, but he must've suspected something.

Perhaps he suspected something again, and like before, was keeping his lips closed over his own suspicions. If so, Susie was doing them all a service by framing Beanpole for his own crime.

The mist thickened into a drizzle when Susie and Emma moved the last of the clothes off of the line. They carried them to the kitchen and put them in a pile on the kitchen counter. Emma said, "I'll spread them out as much as I can around the house until my husband..." She took a breath, blinked, "and my son are home."

"How are they doing?" Susie asked, unwilling to let the opportunity for more information slip away.

"Beanpole killed that Salome Beiler."

Susie flinched. It was no less than the truth, but to hear Emma say it so plainly, her voice edged with anger, felt like a blow.

Susie said, "The judge, and the elders, say it was an accident."

Emma shrugged. "They would know. I always thought Salome Beiler would bring trouble on this house, but not of that sort."

"Salome was a good friend to me," Susie said, her muscles tight as the snake of anger shifted in her chest. Susie did not like Emma Miller, she decided. Before, she had been indifferent to the woman. Sometimes even pitying how hard it must have been for her as a mother, to raise a son like Beanpole. But now, Susie understood. If this was Emma after her therapy, what had she been like before?

Emma shook her head. "Sorry. I did not mean it... I still have problems with my anger."

Susie nodded. "Did it help? Therapy?" Susie asked to break the tension but found she awaited the answer.

Emma nodded. "I still get thoughts, and sometimes I just want to lash out, but it is better than it was, and I can love my husband again without hating him."

Susie nodded.

Emma said, "The hardest part is forgiving

myself. I think I passed that pain to my son. Andrew."

Susie blinked. It was odd to hear Beanpole referred to by his first name. That was what his mother would call him. She asked, "Is Beanpole...well?"

Emma shrugged.

Susie forced a smile. "I came to deliver you a fresh loaf of my cinnamon bread. It is in the buggy."

Emma smiled. She was missing the tooth to the left of her left canine. "Denki. You're a nice girl, Susie Zook. I always thought you were a nice girl. If you had not been so head over heels for Joseph, I wanted you as one of my own."

Susie held her smile through sheer force of will. Inside, she shivered. She could understand why all of Emma's other children had moved far away. One had even fled to the English. Susie went back to the buggy, and, slipping the items she intended to plant in the house inside a second folded up, cloth bag beneath the loaf of bread, Susie returned to the house. The air smelled of detergent and rain. Susie wished she had brought an umbrella. Her hair was damp. At least her winter coat protected her, though drops beat against her forehead and cheeks.

Susie handed over the loaf, removing it from the cloth bag and slipping the bag itself over her shoulder.

Emma said, "We can toast some with butter and have it with some hot tea, if you'd like." Her tone sounded wistful. She was probably lonely.

Susie agreed, and Emma went to the cabinet, pulling down two small plates and taking a knife from a block of wood on the counter.

Emma sliced through the loaf and put both in the oven to warm with a large pad of butter. They sat, the smell of cinnamon wafting out. Emma asked, "You have a daughter, don't you?"

"Margaret, but everyone calls her Greta."

"Yes, she's a quiet one. Beanpole was quiet as a boy. My older two were always talking, talking, talking, but Beanpole, he listened."

The teakettle began to whistle. Susie jumped to her feet. "I can, if you'd like?"

"I only have decaffeinated. Mostly rooibos. It's African, made from a root, so I guess it's not tea at all. But delicious. Caramel vanilla. If you'd like."

"Where is it?"

Emma stood, walked to the counter, and opened the third drawer from the bottom, next to the sink. She began stacking boxes of tea onto the counter, searching for something. After a few moments, she took the bright orange box and said, "This is it. Do you take sugar?"

Susie had she craved sugar when she was pregnant with Margaret, but now, she had reverted to her original tastes. "Just cream, or milk, if it isn't any trouble."

"No trouble." Emma took two mugs, placed tea bags inside, and poured steaming water over the bags to steep. "It will take just a couple of minutes."

Emma had said nothing else disturbing, but their stilted pleasantries still made Susie uncomfortable. Susie wanted to hide the stolen goods in Beanpole's room and get out of here as quickly as she could. Maybe it was the lack of light. Emma had the curtains half drawn, and the outside was gray and raining. Rain beat against the house, and the breeze had the kitchen door rattling. Susie asked, "May I use your bathroom?"

"Downstairs one is small. You can use mine upstairs. Second door to the right.

Susie smiled and thanked her, keeping the cloth bag over her shoulder as she made her way to the stairs. Even with the skylight above, it was dark going up the stairs, and the damp chill seeped into everything. Susie's clothes were still damp from carrying the laundry and running back to her buggy in the rain. Poor Star. The rain was coming down harder now; Perhaps Susie could use her horses an excuse to leave. It was downright cruel to leave him standing out there as the weather worsened.

Susie tiptoed down the hall, cracking open the first door, which revealed a room with twin beds, a pair of quilts folded up at the foot of each, and not much else. The room had a light coating of dust on the nightstand and the table nearest the door. A guest bedroom, Susie surmised. She closed it and went to the next.

On her right, as Emma had promised, was a rest room. Softly, Susie pushed the door shut, tiptoed across the hall, and opened the next door. This one also had a single bed, though it was made up, and a Bible sat on the nightstand. Something red stuck out of it, and Susie, heart pounding, tiptoed closer. A red ribbon, marking a page. She walked over and opened the book.

...if one has a complaint against another, forgiving each other; as the Lord has forgiven you, so you also must forgive.

Colossians 3:13

He would be reading about forgiveness. Susie closed the Bible.

Before she lost her nerve, she opened the night-stand drawer. Inside was an envelope, three bottles of what looked like prescription pills, and a note-book. Was it a journal? Susie closed that drawer, scared to look further, and opened the one beneath.

This one saw less use, as the smell of mothballs and dust attested. Susie took the cross stitch square and pushed it inside, shoving it towards the back. Then, taking an apron she had "borrowed" from Mrs. Fisher, she lifted the mattress and shoved it, wadded up, beneath.

Susie left the room, shutting the door behind her, and was entering the bathroom when she heard the front door to the house open.

Susie's heart pounded. It was, she glanced at her watch, just past four in the afternoon. Could Bean-pole and Jumbo be back? She shut the bathroom door behind her and, in a fit of panic, locked it. Her mouth was dry and her hands were shaking. She sat on the toilet and tried to calm her breathing. After a minute, she flushed the toilet, though she had not used it, and went to the sink to wash her hands.

Below, the sound of footsteps and muffled voices. Emma and a man. Jumbo? Or Beanpole?

Or both? Susie could not determine from the muffled sounds through the door.

Wiping her hands on the skirt of her dress, Susie threw the bag back over her shoulder and, left the bathroom. "Hello," Susie called on the stairs. "I'm coming down!"

As though she had to warn them. As though if Beanpole saw her, he might grab a heavy object and beat her as he had Salome.

The judge said it was an accident, but Susie could not believe. Doctors had studied the bones, determining Salome had taken on a sharp blow to the head. It had likely killed her. Her bones also showed signs of old breaks, though the doctor had claimed those were much older than the head wound. Likely from childhood. But bones could only tell so much of the story. And they could not confirm whether the blow had been accidental. They had only Beanpole's word and the trust of the elders.

As Susie went down the stairs, the voices became clear. Two men. As much as she wanted and prayed to be wrong, she knew it was Jumbo Miller and his son.

Maybe she could just sneak out the front door without speaking to them?

But Jumbo called out, "Who's that upstairs!"

Susie pressed her lips together. An obscenity flashed through her mind, and she begged Gott's forgiveness. "It's me, Susie Zook. I was just dropping off a loaf of bread for your wife. I have to go now. Star. My horse. It's raining." Susie forced herself to stop jabbering like a fool. Susie stopped in the hallway, looking back towards the kitchen at Jumbo speaking and then to the door. Beanpole stood in front of it, taking off his boots.

She would have to pass him to leave. Susie began to shake. Behind her, Jumbo's voice grew louder as his footsteps approached. "That's a right kind gesture, Mrs. Zook. Emma has been lonely, and it was good of you to reach out."

Susie bowed her head. Now she was both scared and ashamed. "I hope you enjoy the bread. I'm sorry I have to leave so quickly."

Susie glanced back towards the door. Beanpole had finished taking off his boots and now he stared at Susie, his lips parted.

Jumbo said, "I'll walk you to the door, Mrs. Zook. You come back and visit again, anytime."

Susie was grateful for Jumbo's presence. She might not have had the courage to pass Beanpole on her own.

"Susie?" Beanpole said as Susie stopped to put her mud-crusted boots on her feet.

"Ja," Susie said. She couldn't look at his face. Her hands were shaking. Beanpole wouldn't attack with his father beside him. He had never been violent in front of witnesses.

If only Salome were here. Salome had always been the brave one. Now, Susie could only be brave in her memory.

It wasn't enough.

Beanpole said, "Sorry. About before. Your daughter talked to me, and… People don't talk to me."

"Margaret is a child."

Beanpole nodded. "She likes chickens. And eggs. And feathers."

"She said all that?" Margaret hardly spoke if she wasn't asked a direct question.

Beanpole nodded. "And she was hungry."

"What did you say to her?" Her voice was sharper than intended, and Susie took another breath. She smiled. "I meant, Margaret does not talk much."

Beanpole shrugged. "I didn't say anything."

Susie finished tying her boots. She said, "I would prefer you not spend time with Margaret outside of my company."

That sounded reasonable, didn't it?

Beanpole nodded, and Jumbo said, "We understand, Mrs. Zook. Beanpole won't be imposing himself anymore. And thank you, again, for your visit."

Susie said her goodbyes and, dipping her head against the rain, ran back to the buggy. Star was soaked, and Susie, feeling guilty, promised her horse a dinner of hot mash and warm blankets after a thorough brushing.

She wasn't sure what to make of Jumbo, Beanpole, and Emma. If she hadn't known their history, she might only have thought Emma odd.

Had she been wrong to plant the stolen goods in Beanpole's room? And how he got Margaret to speak. Was it really so simple as saying nothing?

Beanpole had not seemed menacing, but he had been at home. And even his own father had felt the need to act as a buffer between them. It could be because Susie's fear of Beanpole was obvious.

Susie would not regret what she'd done. Beanpole was a threat to the community. But she also knew she'd crossed the line, and now, there was no going back.

13

*L*uke wished he had picked up some flowers to give to Marion when he stopped at her door, but her face lit up in a beautiful smile when he handed her an umbrella instead. "You think of everything," she said.

Sadie had always said he over-planned and overthought everything. "Loosen up," she had admonished more than once. Yet Marion appreciated Luke's planning. It made Luke smile.

Unfortunately, Luke couldn't just enjoy the moment. Detective Gunter's business card poked through the fabric of his pocket to scratch his thigh. He should show it to Marion and tell her about what had happened.

After the movie. He wasn't even sure Marion

was the same girl. And if she had been there, that didn't mean she'd done anything wrong. He didn't want to ruin things by scaring her off now.

Marion held out her hand, and Luke took it. They walked together, his umbrella shielding hers, to the road where Jerome picked them up.

Kayla sat in the front passenger seat. She was thin with sharp cheekbones, her hair in dozens of tiny braids. She looked up from her phone as they got in, and grinning, said, "You must be Luke and…?"

"Mary," Marion said.

Luke had dressed English for the outing in jeans and a black button-down shirt. He had put gel in his hair to give it an artfully tousled book he'd seen in a magazine.

Marion still dressed Amish, though her borrowed dress was a few inches too short at the sleeves and skirt. Her boots, water stained and worn, were visible up to her ankle. The dress was also a touch tight, making clear the lush curves of her figure, which Luke appreciated. He had traded her old dress for one of his sister's, promising to have it washed on Monday when his mamm and sisters did the laundry.

Kayla said, "Cool. You started working this week at the shop, right?"

Marion nodded. "I'm grateful for the job."

Kayla said, "Jerome says that he can get rude, so watch yourself."

Mary shrugged.

They talked about the movie. Marion slipped her hand onto the seat between them, and Luke took it, a shiver running through him at her closeness. Marion was beautiful. Even in her plain clothing, she stood out. But more than that, she was so nice. At the shop, she made every customer feel special, and as a result, they were more patient with the usual set of mishaps and unexpected problems that came with car repairs.

Luke knew it was foolish, considering everything that had happened, but he could imagine himself and Marion working together and dating for a very long time. He would not let himself think of anything further. Marion was English and squatting. Police detectives were looking for her. No matter how much he helped her, she wouldn't want to live in an abandoned house for the rest of her life. They would have to find a new place to live soon. The Crawleys had hired an English company to maintain the house. Someone would come eventually and see Marion was living there. And then, she would have to go.

Jerome said, "I ordered tickets online. So we don't have to stand in a long line."

Luke thanked him, and Marion asked how much they owed.

Luke said, "I'm paying for your ticket," to Marion.

"But you've done so much for me already!"

"I want to."

Jerome said, "Me too. He smiled at Kayla.

"They had twenty minutes before the movie started, and Kayla suggested getting popcorn.

Marion grinned, eyeing the concessions. Luke, who was indifferent to popcorn, said, "Let's get a large so we can split it. Free refills." Marion had to be hungry, even though they had stopped for lunch on the way home from the shop that afternoon before Luke went to the volleyball game and Marion back to the house. "They have pretzel bites. And hot dogs. Well, pigs in blankets but…"

Marion smiled, taking Luke's hand again. Luke wanted to kiss her. But it would be awkward to do it here in line for concessions. The awkwardness hadn't stopped Jerome from slipping his arm around Kayla's waist however, and she leaned on his shoulder, her eyes half shut as they spoke to each other.

Maybe Luke could put his arm around Marion's waist too? He moved closer to her and she let go his hand, putting her arm around his waist and pulling him closer.

Luke couldn't stop grinning. He felt like he wanted to fly from happiness. Maybe if he were a superhero, like in the movie, he could. But even without powers, Marion made him feel like a hero. Just for being himself.

"Luke!"

Luke's stomach clenched. He looked over his shoulder towards the voice, hoping he was wrong.

Sadie.

Darn.

She stood with two other girls: Fannie from their district, and another he didn't know. All were dressed in English style, for Sadie, tight blue jeans, a low-cut top, her hair unpinned and falling in blonde waves, her lips and cheeks pink and her eyes lined in brown that made the blue sparkle.

Luke forced a smile. Sadie whispered something to Fanny, and then, ignoring the line, walked over to Luke and Marion. Ignoring Jerome, though she knew him and knew he was Luke's friend. She grinned up at Luke. "You clean up well, don't you?"

"Sadie, I'm on a date."

"Yes," she said in the English style. "Yes, you said." Sadie glanced at Marion. Her lips tightened as she took in Marion's face, clothes and hair. She said, "That dress is too small for you and those boots are awful. Luke never noticed my shoes though, so I guess that's working out for you."

Marion smiled, her eyes narrowing. "It is very nice to meet you," she said, not giving her own name. "And I like the look. Those jeans are very…80s."

"I guess your family isn't as strict as you look," Sadie said.

Marion shrugged.

"Or have you run through your English clothes?" Sadie was smiling, but her tone was syrupy acid.

Luke pulled Marion a little closer. "I don't care how Mary dresses. She's beautiful the way she is."

Sadie ignored Luke, fixing her gaze on Marion. "Have we met? What district are you from again?"

"I don't see how that's your business."

"Luke and I are from Bird-in-Hand," Sadie said. "You? Ephrata?"

Marion's expression froze.

From behind the counter, a woman called them forward. "Next!"

"We have to order," Luke said, gratefully.

"Of course. It was a pleasure to meet you, Mary. She leaned a little closer, her voice pitched low. Luke still heard it. Sadie whispered, "Luke thinks all of his girlfriends are perfect, just as they are."

Luke saw red. "Sadie!"

Sadie waved and, grinning, strode back towards her friends.

"I'm sorry," he said to Marion. How could he have thought himself in love with Sadie? She was cruel and now threatened to ruin everything.

"You don't have to apologize for her being a—" Marion clenched her fist. "Witch!"

Kayla burst out laughing.

Jerome clapped Luke on the back. "Out with the old. I always thought Sadie put on a front. A little. Guess it was a lot."

They ordered their popcorn and pretzel bites and sodas and made their way to the theater. Kayla and Jerome made out through most of the previews, and to Luke's surprise, after the third preview,

Marion leaned over and whispered in Luke's ear, "Do you want to kiss me?"

Luke's mouth was dry. "If you'd like." Smooth. Real smooth. "Yeah, I mean."

Marion kissed him on the cheek, or at least tried to, but with their difference in height it was more like his lower jaw.

Luke turned around and kissed her properly. It was slow and sweet and perfect. He wanted to keep kissing her, but the person on his right, a stranger, elbowed him as the opening credits rolled. He took Marion's hand and squeezed it.

Marion smiled, teeth flashing in the light of the flickering screen.

Luke did not remember the movie.

Thankfully, they did not cross paths with Sadie again when leaving the theater.

Jerome, who was now holding hands with Kayla, suggested they stop for burgers and shakes, which they did, cheerfully.

Towards the end of the meal, a pair of uniformed police officers entered and took seats at the counter. Marion shifted her body away from them, so her back was turned as best she could in the booth, and turned her head away even further. She gripped the glass with her now mostly-finished shake, holding the straw to her lips and sucking at the dregs.

Luke leaned over to her and asked, "Are you okay?"

"Yes." Her smile was glass.

Kayla glanced at Marion and then back towards the counter. She swiped a French fry from Jerome's plate and, dipping ketchup, swallowed it whole.

Marion had finished her burger and fries, and most of a shared plate of cheesy nachos.

Of course she was hungry. She couldn't cook at the old Crawley house, and had been living off of snacks and whatever Luke gave her, he assumed. He didn't know.

If Luke was going to take things further with Marion, he needed to learn more about her. Beyond the story the police detective had told. He didn't want her to leave, but he couldn't, in any conscience, court with a girl who might have murdered someone.

Except he was courting with her.

And she hadn't murdered anyone. He would know.

Luke took a sip of his shake. Strawberry. The cold sweetness rested on his tongue, and, hardly hearing the surrounding conversation, he smiled when Kayla said something and Jerome laughed.

Kayla asked, "So how did you two meet?"

Jerome said, "I didn't tell you! It's a crazy story. They met in a haunted house."

"At Halloween?"

Luke shook his head, and Marion said, "A couple of weeks ago."

Luke added, "The house isn't really haunted."

Kayla shrugged. "That's good. When I was a little kid, we moved into a house that was haunted. Not ghosts walking around haunted, but it had a scary feel. I told my mom. And my grandmother got Mrs. Adams in to... Send the spirits on their way, if you know what I mean."

Jerome asked, "Did it work?"

Kayla shook her head. "Mrs. Adams told us to move. Then dad lost his job, and we sold the house. We had to move into a smaller place, and I had to share a room with my sister, but I was all right with that. The old house was scary. Sometimes I had to sleep with the lights on. No joke."

Marion said, "I've never felt scared there." Her gaze unfocused, and she stared out over Kayla's shoulder to the tables beyond. "The house is kind of...comforting..."

Luke's eyes widened. Salome Beiler had died there, and Beanpole Miller had buried her under the oak. Even if the house wasn't haunted, it wasn't comforting. No one had told Mary the story, and maybe it was better that way. Luke didn't believe in ghosts. At least, not seriously. He knew Gott would protect him from harm.

But had Gott protected Salome Beiler?

Had He protected Marion?

Luke finished his shake. At the counter, the two police officers spoke with each other loudly, one laughing.

Luke said, "I think they're just on their break."

They finished eating and paid the bill. The two officers left just ahead of them, one, a stocky man with short, brown hair, held the door open.

Luke thanked him and the others followed. Marion kept her face angled downwards, bringing her fingers up to stroke her cheekbone just beneath her eye. The gesture covered most of her face with her hand. Luke, recognizing her fear, stepped forward, using his body to obstruct her from view.

Once they were back in the car, Kayla glanced at her watch. Jerome," she said, glancing at her watch. "I have to be home by 11:30."

Luke said, "You can drop us where you picked us up."

"On the side of the road?" Kayla asked, her voice tinged with obvious surprise. "Jerome can drop you off at your houses."

Marion paled.

Luke said, "Mary's family is strict," he added, though how that explained anything, he couldn't even say. "I'll walk Mary to her house. It isn't far from the road."

"If you're sure?" Kayla said, twisting in the seat to look at them.

Luke glanced at Marion again. She pressed her lips together. Luke nodded. "It's better that way."

Kayla said, "That sucks about your parents, Mary."

Marion shrugged.

Jerome said something about the movie, and they chatted until Jerome slowed down by the side of the two-lane road where he picked up Luke, and now Marion, every morning.

Kayla said, "I was nice to meet you, Mary, Luke."

Marion smiled, and she said, "You too. Maybe we can do this again—" She bit the edge of her lower lip. "I mean, if we can."

"Yeah," Kayla said.

Luke took Marion's hand as they both waved as Jerome pulled his car away, the back lights fading into the distance.

"Thank you," Marion said. "For everything."

"Let me walk you back," Luke said.

Marion smiled, and her face in the half moon's light, made his heart pound. He loved the warmth of her hand in his. He wanted to kiss her again. At the same time, he was scared. Not of kissing her, but of losing her.

Salome might not haunt the Crawley house, but Marion was like a ghost. She could vanish just as easily as she had appeared. Luke didn't know where she was going. He doubted she knew either.

And because she was running from something, if it caught up to her, she would run again.

The air was chilly and damp with the scent of rain. He wished he could just enjoy the moment, the walk, her hand in his and the promise of a goodnight kiss. But Luke wasn't the type to pretend the future didn't exist. He was uptight, as Sadie used to say, and always planning. It was true. Luke had contingencies for everything. Even here, he had hidden an umbrella by the side of the road, in the low scrub next the trees, just in case he forgot one in the morning and it started to rain on his drive home. He kept extra sandwich fixings in the shop fridge. Just in case. Except for with Marion, Luke didn't take risks.

With her, he was risking everything.

They reached her borrowed home.

Marion said, "It was really fun tonight, thank you."

"I had a good time too. And I like you..." Luke took a breath. "But I need you to tell me the truth. About Timothy Eldridge."

Marion pulled her hand from his. "What? About—who?"

"You were there. When he died."

"I should go."

"Two cops came by the volleyball game today. A local officer and a detective from Philadelphia. She had a picture. It was hard to see, but I think it was of you."

Marion took a step back. "What did you tell them?"

"Nothing! They said you might have had something to do with a murder."

"No!" Marion massaged her left palm with the thumb of her right hand. "I—" She swallowed. Breathed. "I didn't kill him. I tried to help."

"Then you should tell them what you saw." He reached into his pocket for the business card. "The detective gave me this. You should call her." He pushed it into her hand.

"They won't believe me." Marion crumpled the card in her hand. She swallowed a sob. "Nobody believes me. Is there a bus station around here? But they'll be checking the buses."

"Don't cry," Luke said, stepping closer to her, so she was facing him, so he could see her.

Marion lowered her head. "I'm sorry."

"I believe you." Luke cupped her jaw and, fingers damp, gently pressed his lips to her forehead.

"I shouldn't have gotten you mixed up in this. Maybe it's best if I just stay gone." Marion sobbed. "I'm already a squatter. And a thief. And a liar."

"You're a good person." Luke pulled her close, wrapping his arms around her as she sobbed against his chest. Anger, slow and hot, burned through him. Marion treated people with kindness, and she hadn't taken a thing from Mr. Johnson, even though she'd run the register the past three days. All she needed was some help from someone who cared.

Luke cared. Maybe too much. He couldn't stand to see her hurting like this.

"You don't even know my real name," she breathed into his shoulder.

"Tell me."

A long silence. She whispered, "Maryanne."

"I love that name."

"I've messed up your shirt," she said, pulling away.

He took both of her hands. "I don't care about the shirt."

Maryanne said, "You may be the best thing that has ever happened to me."

Luke's skin warmed. He squeezed her hands. "I can't. I mean, I can't be."

Maryanne pulled on his hands, stepping to him and then, getting up on her toes, she pressed a kiss to his lips. It was a quick peck, but then she let go and slipped her arms around his chest. They kissed again, slower and deeper. Her lips tasted of salt, it mingled with the sweetness of her mouth and the emotion growing inside of him. Luke wanted to protect her. He wanted to be with her tomorrow, and the next day. He would hold her for as long as he could. Maryanne was a warm, beautiful ghost in his arms. Luke might not keep her in his life, but for now, he could kiss her.

Luke kissed her forehead. Maryanne kissed his cheek. He kissed her ear. She kissed his chin. They kissed each other's lips again.

They kissed until it threatened to become more than kissing, and then Luke stepped back and ran his hand through his hair. "I... Um..." He felt cold and empty without her in his arms. His body, and his heart, wanted to hold her again. "Tomorrow is Sunday and I will be with my family."

She nodded. "Of course. Yes. Thank you. For everything."

"Don't leave me. We'll figure something out. I promise. Just don't run again, okay? Please."

"I won't run," she said. They kissed a final time, and she slipped back into the house, the door clicking shut.

Luke stood alone on the battered porch. He wanted to knock and even raised a hand to do so, just so he could see her again. But no. He could not risk losing control with her. Especially not now, when she was finally beginning to trust him for real.

At the edge of the trees Luke looked back at the dark house. One day, Luke prayed, Maryanne would trust him enough to tell her story.

14

*M*aryanne had stayed awake late into the night. She didn't deserve Luke. He was so kind. Her body thrilled at his kisses, but her soul was drawn to his steadiness. He really was a hero. If that other girl, the one who had been so fake nice but underneath rancid and nasty, was his ex, maybe Luke was just a hero with a knack for choosing the wrong women.

Marion curled up in a pallet of old clothes, two pillows, one she had stolen and one Luke had given her along with a heavy Amish quilt. The attic, thankfully, had stored a single mattress. It was sized for a ten-year-old child, but far better than sleeping on the hard wooden floor.

With Luke's help, Maryanne had made her

second floor "apartment" quite cozy. She had a flashlight, a bag of hand and foot warmers, another stash of candy bars, and some sodas, and even a dog-eared paperback which Christine had lent her.

Maybe Maryanne could make a life here. Not in this abandoned house, but among the Amish. With Luke. She could erase Maryanne and just be Mary, Luke's girlfriend. Or wife?

No. She was way too young to be thinking about being somebody's wife.

Eventually, Maryanne slept.

Maryanne woke to the rumble of an approaching car engine. She sat bolt upright. A car? Here?

Her mouth went dry. Quickly, she folded up the blanket and shoved it along with the mattress into the closet. Hopefully, whoever was coming would not look up here. Then she grabbed her snacks and her flashlight and everything else around her and shoved it into her backpack.

She had just finished this when she heard the rattle of the front door opening.

At least she had remembered to lock the door this time, unlike when the boys had come.

Unfortunately, she was now trapped.

Whoever had entered had a key, which meant

they might be the owner. Or someone hired by the owner. Whoever they were, they would recognize Maryanne didn't belong and call the police.

Marion, backpack slung over her shoulder, tiptoed down the hall.

From downstairs, she heard a male voice. He spoke and waited as though listening for a response. Cellphone. It had to be.

Maryanne and looked up and down the hall. She could hide at the far end, crouched down, and hope he went straight upstairs towards the back rooms first. Then she could make a break for the stairs.

It was a fifty-fifty chance. But better to try. As he came up the stairs, his back would be to her and he would have to turn around to walk down the section of the hall.

Decision made, Maryanne dropped into a crouch. Maybe he wouldn't notice her dishes in the sink. She should have put them in the cabinet. Stupid!

From where she hid, the voice on the phone was clearer than it had been on the other side of the hall.

"Billy! I think you've got a squatter."

Maryanne's heart pounded.

"See if the cleaning service left this stuff here and call me back. If it is not them then…" The man's voice faded as he passed the stairs to the kitchen.

He was pacing. After another fifteen seconds, the footsteps returned, and she heard him say, "If there is someone swatting here, I'd rather wait for the cops. I've got a baseball bat in my car though, if anything gets out of hand."

Another pause and then laughter.

Marion was shaking. Maybe she should go back to one of the rooms and lock the door. But if he brought the police, they could just knock it down.

His footsteps faded and returned. "All right. All right, I'll go back to the car."

A few seconds later, the front door shut again. Maryanne waited, just trying to breathe. She had to move. If he was sitting in the car, maybe she could sneak out through the kitchen door. But what if he was watching? The driveway was in front of the house. The kitchen in the back. But she would have to cross the yard to get away. He would see her for sure then.

But she couldn't stay here. If the cops found her squatting, they would put her in jail for sure. And then Bobby would get her. Or arrange someone to get her. Bobby had already killed one guy and covered up the death of another woman.

Luke was right. Maryanne should have come forward before instead of hiding here. She couldn't afford to get arrested now. Luke had said he would help her, and she trusted him.

But first, she had to get out of the house.

The longer she waited, the more likely they would discover her. Maryanne took three calming breaths and slung her backpack over her shoulders. Heart pounding, she tiptoed down the stairs and dropped to her knees, crawling along the floor towards the kitchen. If she stayed low to the ground, the man in the car would not see her through the windows.

Maryanne was in her Amish dress, so if he came back and caught her, the dress might make the guy think twice about hitting her with a bat.

She crawled to the kitchen door and reached up towards the knob. It was locked. Slowly, she turned the inside lock. The light clicks sounded like a hammer on metal. Her heart pounded in her ears as she waited, holding her breath, but no sound. She turned the knob and opened the door. There was another door, a screen door, and she reached up, unlatching it and pushing it open an inch to peer out through the gap.

Nothing in her direct vision, but if he was parked to the left instead of the right, she would not see him. If he had parked out front in the driveway, and he stayed inside the car now, then maybe she had a chance. The door was not visible from the front of the house. But if he had come around back to catch the squatter leaving, then she would run straight into his arms. Or into his bat.

She pushed the door open a little further. A bird let out a trill of tweets.

The sound mingled with the ring of discordant chimes, heard from where they hung on the front porch. It was sunny, at least, though Maryanne would have preferred thick clouds and fog. Fog would be great. As it was, if she dashed across the yard, he would see her for sure.

Her best bet was to go down the kitchen stairs and hide beneath them until the police entered the house. Then, while they were occupied searching, she could make a run for it. Hopefully, nobody would be outside. But even if they were, they might hesitate at her Amish clothing.

It was a terrible plan, but Maryanne didn't have a better one. She pushed the door open further, enough for her to crawl outside. Then, she pulled the kitchen door shut. She couldn't block it from outside. She didn't have a key. It had been pure luck the back door had been unlocked when she found the place.

Slowly, very slowly, she eased the screen door shut.

In the distance, the sound of sirens.

Not bothering to climb down the stairs, Maryanne hopped from the narrow ledge, not quite a deck, to the ground and then, clutching her flashlight, hid beneath the stairs as the sirens grew louder.

She waited.

Maryanne kept herself as still as she could. She should have worked out a plan for when someone came to look at the house. She could have hidden her things and then come back later. Instead, she'd left most everything there, evidence of her squatting. At least she had her backpack and the rest of the cash Mr. Johnson had paid her.

At least Maryanne had kept the place clean. Maybe, if they caught her, she could be forgiven because she had done that.

The siren cut. Maryanne heard the rumble of a second motor before the car parked.

Voices, distorted by distance. The sound of footsteps. Maryanne had expected them to take the front entrance, but they approached the kitchen stairs. Maryanne held her breath.

"Looks like a regular squatter, officer," a man said. She recognized his voice as the same man from earlier who had been speaking on the cellphone. He asked, "You think it's that girl?"

"Could be," a second man, his voice low and gravelly. "We contacted Detective Gunter."

The two men climbed up the stairs, shaking dust onto Maryanne's head. She held her breath.

The kitchen door rattled open, and they walked inside.

Luke had said a detective was in the area looking for her. Maryanne had thought, for a moment, she might be safe. But she wasn't safe anywhere. Her parents and brother had died in a car accident. Her aunt had taken her boyfriend's side when Maryanne explained how Billy had tried to touch her. And then Tim. Dead. How long until she joined him?

Maryanne clutched her hands together. She hadn't prayed since she was a little girl. She wasn't even sure if she believed in God, but now, she could only hope he believed in her enough to listen.

"God, please, help me get out of here. I'll do better. I promise."

Maryanne shook her head. Even if there was a God, he would not help Maryanne out of this mess. She should have stayed with Tim until the ambulance came. Maybe he'd be alive. Or maybe he'd be dead, but she'd have been able to tell them who killed him. She'd run, lived for almost two weeks in this house without permission, stolen and lied, and now, she would pay the price. This was all her fault.

After the door shut, Maryanne counted to sixty.

Maryanne had to run.

Now.

But Maryanne couldn't move. Her legs were held down by heavy weights. She couldn't breathe. Couldn't think. She hugged her arms around her legs. Maybe she could wait until after they left.

Or maybe it didn't matter what she did. Maybe she had already lost.

15

Two days after Susie had planted the stolen goods in Beanpole's room, Hannah came by to talk about Mrs. Stoltzfus' missing cross-stitch. It had been a treasure to Mrs. Stoltzfus. Her mother's, stitched by her sister who had then left their community and become English. Susie's stomach roiled at the news. She felt more and more the sinner. With malice and forethought, Susie had stolen something precious from Mrs. Stoltzfus.

Yes, her intentions had been to help the community, but the road to hell was paved with such intentions. If only Susie had found another way.

Susie asked, "Does anyone know who might be responsible?"

Hannah shook her head. "My uncle is saying that we may wish to call in the English police. Though we dislike them mixing in our affairs. But what if it is a vagrant? If so, their actions are growing more and more severe."

"How so?" Susie had asked.

"It is one thing to steal a pan or some eggs, but to take that cross-stitch, that speaks more to avarice than desperation."

It did. And Susie carried that on her shoulders.

Maybe it would be better to confess and accept her penance. But then, her theft would be for nothing. Beanpole would still be in the community, and Susie would risk her own place. Risk losing her family.

No. She had to follow through.

Are you sure it's a vagrant?" Susie asked.

"What else could it be?"

Susie shrugged. If she suggested Beanpole, it would be too obvious. The goods had gone missing right after Susie's visit, and Susie's path went from Mrs. Stoltzfus's house to the Miller's home.

Hannah said, "Be careful. Whoever it is… Possessions are only possessions, but if this person is brazen enough to break into our homes and rob us, imagine if we stumble across him! Who knows what he might do?"

Susie nodded. "Thank you for warning me," she said.

"It was the least I could do, considering how kind you've been. And how open you've been to me about your..." She rubbed her rounding belly. "I cannot talk to my husband about this, and my mother is more traditional. She gives me herbs and said everything will be fine and that it is better not to talk about it because a child is a blessing and by Gott's hand, all will be made right. She was not so devout before Daed passed, but after she came through her dark place, she leans on Gott in all things." Hannah shook her head. "I know this is the right thing to do, to have faith, but I worry about the baby."

"You can talk to me," Susie said. "There are small things which have little to do with the baby's health, but are important to know about and know are normal. If you have any questions, ask."

Hannah took Susie's hands, eyes shining. "I wish I could be as good as you."

Tears rose to Susie's eyes. "I am not so good."

"You would say that!"

The confession rested on Susie's tongue, and she swallowed it down. Hannah would do better to follow her mother's example. But Susie understood how alone a woman could feel, having to keep the transitions of her pregnancy to herself.

Susie's mamm had been open about being "with child" but only in the most general senses. Susie had weathered her miscarriage on her own. She was grateful Joe was less reserved than many Amish men were about pregnancy. He had even visited the fertility doctor with Susie, as embarrassing as it had been, and though he would not be unfaithful to her by taking part in some of the tests they required, he stood by her side and he did not pretend her pregnancy was something apart from him.

Hannah stayed a half-hour longer before needing to go home and cook dinner for her husband. It was a clear, crisp afternoon, perfect weather for a walk. Susie called to Margaret, and she bounded to get her coat and boots on.

As Susie and Margaret walked along the driveway towards the edge of the field, frost crunched under her boots. This was the sort of day Salome loved. She'd enjoyed walking with her hands in the pockets of her jacket and a long scarf twined around her neck. She'd hated gloves. So did

Margaret, who usually pulled them off and let them hang from the long elastic band Susie had clipped to each and pushed through the sleeves of her daughter's coat to keep her from losing them.

Margaret dashed off ahead.

Joe would be back for dinner. Susie had left half of a potpie in the refrigerator to reheat. Joe liked leftovers. And he loved potpie. Maybe they could go to Joe's father's barn and visit him and his father. Susie wished she had thought to bring some snacks, but their smiling faces would be enough. And she and Margaret could ride back with Joe in the buggy if Margaret got too tired.

Plan set, Susie walked and let her mind wander.

Margaret ran back, clutching a small, gnarled twig and, with a bright smile, handing it to Susie.

"What's this?" Susie asked.

Margaret wrinkled her nose. "Twig."

And she really chattered on and on with Beanpole? Susie couldn't imagine it. Getting a few words, let alone a sentence, out of her daughter was pulling teeth.

The second time Margaret returned with a crocus bud. Susie smiled.

"It's a flower," Margaret said, speaking in a complete sentence, to Susie's delight.

"A beautiful flower," Susie said, smiling. She loved her home and her family. As they walked, the weight of her sins lightened, and she just enjoyed the sun.

Margaret dashed ahead again, running onto a small path that branched left from the edge of the narrow path along the edge of the field.

"Ne!" Susie yelled. "Come back!" Though it was at least a mile down the road and beyond a second fork, that path went towards the old Crawley house where Salome had died.

Margaret froze. "Mamm!" she screamed.

Susie ran to her daughter.

Margaret pointed into the trees on the opposite side.

"What's wrong?" Susie asked.

Margaret pointed.

Susie's heart pounded. It was probably just an animal, or an oddly shaped tree, but Margaret's wide eyes, and the fact she was still, made Susie fear it was something worse.

Margaret said, "Lady."

Susie squinted into the trees. "What lady?"

"Hiding." Margaret pointed again.

"Come on out!" Susie called.

Nothing. Three large tree trunks obscured the

distance ahead of them, and one large rock. At the edge, she glimpsed the side of a hand and the top of what looked like a prayer kapp. Someone *was* hiding. As Margaret had said, a lady.

Was this the vagrant?"

Thoughts of Salome, fleeing her home and hiding in the woods near a strange district, made Susie's stomach churn. She picked up Margaret and walked towards the trees. "It's okay. I'm not going to hurt you," she said. "Do you need help?"

There was no reason to assume the girl was in trouble. She might have been enjoying an afternoon with a boy and feared being caught. Out of politeness, Susie should take Margaret and leave the girl to it, but something inside insisted this girl needed help. So Susie continued towards her. "Just yell so I know you haven't hurt yourself."

From behind the rock, a young woman's voice, "I'm fine!"

She sounded strange, and Susie realized it was her accent; she sounded English.

The missing dresses, stolen food and the quilt made a sudden sense. This wasn't an Amish girl in trouble. It was an English girl. The vagrant.

This made it more imperative that Susie find out what she intended before she revealed herself to any of the others. The point of stealing the other items wasn't to pin it on this girl. Susie needed the elders to blame Beanpole for all the thefts.

"You can stand up, if you want to." Susie shifted Margaret on her hip. "It's easier to talk to a person than the side of a rock."

"I'm sorry," the girl said, confirming Susie's intuition that she was likely English. Amish people, as a habit from Pennsylvania Dutch, simply said "sorry," and dropped the "I'm, or I am."

The girl stood. Her prayer cap hung from the side of her head, and she had her hair pulled back in a bun not fixed with pins, but with the lumpy outline of a large, English style hair tie. The dress was too large on her, the apron tied twice around her waist.

Susie's asked, "What's your name?"

The girl wiped her damp, muddy palms on the side of her dress, avoiding the dirt-smudged apron. "Mary," she added, her voice taking on a more Amish lilt. "My name is Mary."

Now that she was affecting it, Mary's accent was excellent. She carried a backpack over her shoulders.

Susie asked, as though she had run across Mary

on an afternoon stroll as opposed to hiding behind a rock, "Which way were you heading?"

Mary pointed behind Susie, the way she had come.

Now that Susie could see Mary in the full light, she noted that while the girl's dress was muddy, her skin was clean for someone who had been skulking around, stealing food from neighboring homes. Had she snuck into a house and taken a bath while no one was home?

This seemed unlikely. Amish families were large, and houses were rarely empty.

Except the Crawley house. Some kids had claimed they saw something moving around inside. A ghost.

Susie suspected she was looking at that ghost right now.

Susie walked closer, and before the girl could object, Susie linked her arm through Mary's. If Mary had been Amish, a shock of such a personal gesture would have surprised her. But Mary accepted it. She glanced behind her.

"Are you okay?" Susie asked.

"Ja," Mary said. "I should be going."

Susie said, "It looks like you could use some help. We have room for one more at our dinner table tonight, if you would like to join my husband and me."

She spoke without thinking and immediately questioned herself. Joe would not be happy to have this girl in their home. Mary was pretending to be Amish. She could be dangerous, and now Susie was inviting her into their home. At the same time, something about the girl's fear, her dark hair, eyes and the brittleness of her smile reminded Susie of Salome.

If Salome had been running from something, could Susie have ignored her pain? Maybe if someone had stopped to help Salome, she might still be alive.

Also, Susie couldn't let anyone else discover this girl's thefts. It would ruin the plan.

It was only good fortune Susie had discovered Mary first.

Susie said, "This is Margaret, my daughter."

Mary smiled and held out her hand. "Nice to meet you," she said.

Margaret looked at the girl's hand and back at Susie.

"Go ahead," Susie said. "She'll show you."

Margaret held out her hand and Mary took it. Margaret smiled.

"What do you say?" Susie encouraged her daughter.

"Hi," Margaret said.

Mary burst out laughing.

Susie smiled too. Mary couldn't have been older than 17. What was she running from? Susie said, "Come. We're having chicken potpie and apple casserole for dessert."

Mary bit her lower lip. "I shouldn't," she said.

"Your parents?" Susie, hoping the girl would agree to this offer, added "Joe's father has a phone in his barn, if you want to let them know you're okay."

Mary shook her head, and her right fist clenched. "No."

So Mary had run away from home. Susie's heart went out to her. Salome ran away when they were both eleven years old. She had hidden in Susie's barn until Susie's older brother discovered the girl on a pallet behind the horses. It had been summer, and the weather warm. Susie brought her friend leftovers from their meals and left the door unlocked so Salome could sneak in and use the toilet at night.

The ruse had lasted for three days. Susie's parents had punished her with lectures and extra chores. Salome hadn't come out again for a week. And when she had, she hunched in on herself, her right arm cradling her lower chest as though it hurt to move.

No one had spoken of that either.

"It's only dinner," Susie said. And after dinner, Susie would offer Mary the spare bedroom. Though how she would justify it, she didn't know.

Mary rifled through her bag. "I'm happy to chip in. I don't want to be any trouble." Mary added, "I have a job."

Mary looked back down the road.

Susie said, "That way's the old Crawley house. Englishers maintain it now. We don't know anything about them."

Mary swallowed and shifted her backpack on her shoulder. "Thank you," she said.

Margaret tugged on Mary's skirt and pointed towards the trees, where a blue jay spread its wings and began to trill.

Mary smiled. "That's a blue jay."

"Pretty!"

"I'm glad for the company. You're doing me a favor."

"I am?" She scratched the back of her neck.

"Margaret needs someone to talk to."

When they got back to the house, Susie had Mary put her knapsack on the sofa in the front room and, deciding to keep the girl too busy to run again, she had her wash her hands and help with chores inside the house.

Mary went about her work happily, even singing a little under her breath, a song Susie remembered hearing in Tiffany's car the week before.

Susie was careful not to ask Mary anything about herself or her family. If she'd been hiding in the old Crawley house, she wanted to get away from something. And since Susie needed her to stay long enough for Beanpole to take the blame for all the thefts, it would be best not to scare her off.

They worked and prepared dinner, a roast Susie had intended to use the next week but now, with Mary here, the extra food would be helpful. As the meat baked and sides warmed in the oven, Susie asked Mary, "Do you quilt?"

Mary shook her head. "I have a quilt. Amish. I — A friend gave it to me."

So Susie was not the only Amish person who knew about Mary. Was it Beanpole? Mary was alive, so it had to be someone else.

Either that, or Beanpole had been truthful when he'd said he had tried to help Salome.

Or maybe Beanpole's medication was working, for now, and Mary had just been lucky to avoid his wrath.

It was too much to think about.

Mary and Margaret hit it off, which allowed Susie to relax a little. Susie pretended not to hear Mary's questions to Margaret about how they stored their food, "You have a refrigerator?" and what words they used for grace, at which, to Susie's shock, her daughter recited the first two lines of the Lord's Prayer and then added, "but you can be quiet."

Joe came home as Mary and Margaret were setting the table. Upon hearing the door, Susie left the kitchen and quickly went to the front door to greet her husband and warn him they had a guest.

Joe kissed her and then said, "Is that roast? It smells gutt."

Susie smiled. "Ja. And we have a guest."

"We do?"

"Her name is Mary. She's visiting our district, and I asked if she could join us for dinner. She's helping Margaret now."

Joe's brow furrowed. He pulled his coat off and turned to hang it on the hook. "Just now? On a

Sunday? I think the elders might have given us some notice."

Susie said, "I ran into her with Margaret. We were taking a walk. She's sweet, and because it is Sunday, especially, I felt it important we offer her dinner at least."

"And her family?"

"I don't know. She is of rumspringa age." Though not on rumspringa. Susie wasn't sure if she should share that Mary was likely the vagrant, now hiding here. She decided to keep her mouth shut. Even sharing this with her husband endangered all she had done to stop Beanpole. Instead, she forced a smile and pointed at the bench next to the coat hook, "Did you want me to help you get your boots off?"

"You're changing the subject."

"I am. Let us have a pleasant meal. Please."

The sound of something hitting the kitchen floor, and then a wail. Susie dashed towards the sound. "Margaret!"

Mary stood between Margaret and what looked like a shattered glass.

Margaret said, "I—" She sobbed. "I dropped it."

Mary smiled at her. "It's okay. It's only a glass."

Susie said, "I'll get the broom and dust pan."

When she returned, Mary had Margaret in the corner of the dining room, far from the broken glass. Mary knelt to Margaret's height, and stuck her thumbs in ears, fingers waving as she made a face.

Margaret laughed. Her face was still wet with tears, but the guilt and sadness had passed.

Susie said, "Thank you, Mary." She said in the English style, just to be certain that the girl understood.

Joe stood at the doorway to the room, his arms folded as he leaned against the doorframe. He glanced at Susie who nodded before kneeling to sweep up the pieces of broken glass.

Joe said, "You're good with kids, Miss."

Mary looked up. Her eyes widened. "Denki, sir," she said in a good imitation of their accent.

Joe asked, "Do you have brothers and sisters?"

Mary flinched. "A brother. I did. He's gone now. Passed on."

"My condolences."

"I miss him," Mary said, averting her gaze to the floor. "Can I help with the glass?"

Joe glanced at Susie who gave a faint shrug with one shoulder as she continued sweeping. Mary could have mentioned a brother's death for sympathy, but Susie didn't think so. The girl had seemed uncomfortable, and Susie didn't want to cause her further pain. She couldn't help wondering, though, where Mary's parents were. Had Mary run away? Why?

Perhaps, like Salome, Mary had good reasons. If so, Susie was glad to help. It was an atonement. The kindness would not balance the weight of Susie's sins, but it was something.

When the glass was swept up and replaced, they sat around the table to eat. Mary reached for her fork, and then glanced across the table to Susie, who closed her eyes and bowed her head.

Joseph gave the blessing for the meal, and they ate.

For the first few minutes, it was silence and appreciative noises, the scrape of fork tines on dishware as they ate.

Joe said, "Gutt, very gutt, wife."

Mary, cocking her head for a second after Joseph spoke, added, "Ja! Very gutt!"

She did sound Amish.

Either Mary had a great ear, or she had spent some time around other Amish people. She had mentioned having received a quilt from a friend.

Maybe that was why she had hidden here with the Amish. Why she had not stayed with her friend still baffled Susie. Why hide at the old Crawley house?

"Denki," Susie said.

When they finished the meal, Joe leaned back in his chair, patting his belly with a contented sigh.

Mary said, "Denki again for inviting me for dinner, Mrs. Zook."

Susie smiled, "I told you to call me Susie, Mary."

"Susie."

Joe asked, "Whereabouts are you staying?"

Mary bit her lower lip. "With friends. I... We... Had a falling out, so I was going to..." She shrugged. "You have helped me a lot." She swallowed, and her eyes shone. Susie feared the girl might burst into tears. "I don't want to impose."

The sun had long ago set, and it was nearing eight at night. Susie glanced at Joe. "We have a spare room..."

Joe said, "A moment, please. I need to speak with my wife."

Mary jumped to her feet. "I'm fine. I'll be fine. Don't fight!"

Joseph said, "Sit down. Keep an eye on Margaret. Will you do that?"

Mary nodded.

Susie smiled. "We will just be a minute. You can have more of the apple pastry.

Margaret, who had begun to nod off, opened her eyes and asked, "Ice cream?"

"It's in the freezer."

Mary nodded and held out her hand to Margaret, who took it.

Susie followed her husband to the front room. Mary's knapsack sat on the couch. Susie figured the girl wouldn't try to leave without it, so it was safe enough to leave her. Besides, vagrant or no, Mary was a sincere girl. And she hadn't stolen anything. Not even a five-dollar bill Susie had left deliberately on the counter earlier when leaving Mary to chop vegetables while Susie and Margaret went upstairs to set up the guest room, just in case.

Joe whispered, "I know you wish to offer kindness, Susie, but we know nothing about this girl."

Susie said, "Mary needs our help." She explained about how Mary had not touched the money on the counter and how she had helped around the house and been good with Margaret, who liked her. "Mary has nowhere to go. And she's scared. I should think if someone discovered our daughter in a similar situation—"

"Our daughter would never be in such a situation!"

"We do not know what Gott plans for our futures. Heaven forbid, we could become ill or even pass before Margaret is married or old enough to support herself. The Lord tells us to be kind to the stranger. This is our test."

"Susie..." Joe sighed, and his shoulders slumped. "Is Mary even Amish?"

Susie shrugged. "Does it matter?"

Joseph rested his hand on Susie shoulders and looked down. "You are a good woman, Susie."

Susie's face flamed. She was not a good woman. At least, not in this.

Susie closed her eyes. *Dear Gott, make me the woman Joseph sees. Don't let my sins be in vain and forgive me them.*

Even as Susie lacked the ability to forgive herself or Beanpole?

Joe said, "Mary will stay the night. We shall see from there in the morning."

16

---

*M*aryanne wanted to cry in gratitude at the generosity of the Zook family. Susie Zook just accepted her, invited her for dinner, a stranger, and now, belly full, Mary wondered what to do next.

Maybe she should pray again. It had worked before, at the house.

What if Mr. Zook sent Maryanne away?

It made sense.

Why else would Mr. Zook drag Mrs. Zook into another room so they could whisper together? He couldn't want Maryanne to stay the night. They had a young child. Maryanne could be an ax murderer. Or just a regular murderer.

If they knew the police were looking for

Maryanne, would they turn her in? Amish people didn't have cellphones. That was the only thing that kept her from running away right now.

Maryanne had stolen from this community.

Now that she had a job, she should try to pay the people back for what she had taken. It was the least she could do.

At the table, Margaret twisted in her chair, placing her palms on the table and maneuvering herself so she could stand and reach for the pan of apple pastry.

"No!" Maryanne whispered, standing and putting a steadying palm on the little girl's back so she wouldn't fall. "Sit down. I'll get you more."

Margaret nodded. Maryanne did as she had promised, taking the last two square pieces of the pastry and giving Margaret the larger one.

Margaret gave Maryanne an impish grin and before Maryanne could do anything, the little girl leaned forward and switched their plates. "You're a guest," Margaret said.

Maryanne swallowed down tears. "You are so sweet."

Margaret took a spoonful of the pastry and shoved it into her mouth. Then she shook her head and pointed down at the rest on her plate. "Sweet," she sputtered, mouth full.

Maryanne smiled and took another bite of the pastry. Even though she was full, who knew when she would next eat a meal this good? And if she had to sleep outside, which she might, at least she was full, and it would be easier to stay warm.

If only she'd been able to grab the quilt Luke had given her. She had nothing to remember him by. How was she even going to meet up with him and Jerome? She vaguely remembered the route they had taken, but she had always followed Luke, and they had always started from the Crawley house. Now Maryanne would have to sneak almost back to it and then retrace her steps around the cornfield and down the narrow path through the trees to the road.

Worse, she wasn't even sure what time she was supposed to meet with them. She'd always woken up with the sun and then waited for Luke to come. She didn't have a watch, and her phone was dead.

Maybe if she just got up at dawn, and ran there, she would be okay.

Since she would probably be sleeping outside, maybe she should find it tonight and then just sleep there.

The thought of sleeping outside scared Maryanne. What if some murderer driving by in his car saw her as easy prey? Or one of Mr. Dobbs' goons. Or what if coyotes attacked her? Did coyotes live around here or foxes? Which ones ate people?

Maryanne took another bite of her dessert. Hot flaky crust and cinnamon apples. She could weep with delight. It was weird eating by flickering lantern light, but it didn't matter. People said the Amish lived simply, but they had a refrigerator, working stove and running water. After having spent the past two weeks living in an abandoned house, this was the lap of luxury. She didn't have to bring water from the creek to flush the toilet, or refill her plastic jug with water from the gas-station bathroom.

Maybe, if Maryanne offered the Zooks money, they would let her stay overnight. She knew she couldn't expect anything long term, but if she could stay overnight, then she could get up and go to work in the morning and talk to Luke or Christine or Jerome. If she could crash on Christine or Jerome's couch, at least long enough to meet with the reporter. If he even accepted her story.

Maryanne couldn't leave Luke without saying goodbye.

Luke made her feel like she mattered for herself.

Maryanne glanced back at the doorway to the hallway. She couldn't hear Mr. and Mrs. Zook talking, but it had to be about her. What if they wanted to call the cops? Maryanne would have to run.

Not yet. She hoped, not yet.

Margaret asked, "Do you like chickens?"

"What kind of chickens?" On these farms, she'd seen chickens walking around and a rooster would have pecked her within an inch of her life once if she hadn't got back over the fence. "Roosters are mean," Maryanne said.

Margaret nodded solemnly. "I like hens."

"Hens are cute," Maryanne said, albeit having limited experience of them. "They lay eggs."

"I like eggs a lot."

"How do you like them? Scrambled? Hard-boiled?"

"Sunshine."

Marion smiled. "Sunnyside up?"

Margaret nodded with a smile.

"How about over easy?"

Margaret cocked her head, brow furrowed, and gave a little slow nod.

"Over light?"

"What's over light?"

"It's like over easy but runny. You don't see the sunny part."

Margaret nodded again. "I like the sunny part," she said.

Marion said, "The sunny part is the best."

Mr. and Mrs. Zook returned. Maryanne looked up from her plate. Husband and wife were framed in the doorway. Mrs. Zook smiled, and Maryanne breathed out a sigh of relief.

Mrs. Zook said, "Thank you so much for joining us for dinner. Margaret and you are having quite a conversation."

Marion smiled back. "We like eggs."

Margaret nodded.

Mrs. Zook glanced at her husband. "Joe, Margaret hardly talks for most people."

Maryanne shrugged. "Margaret is an excellent conversationalist."

"Joe?"

Mr. Zook nodded, "My wife says you're passing through, and you don't have a place to stay right now."

Marion said, "I have a job. I can pay, just tell me how much."

Joe's eyes narrowed. "You have a job?"

"It's new. I was going to stay in a hotel,"

Maryanne lied. She couldn't stay in a hotel. Not with the police looking for her. "But I don't have a car, you understand." Of course he understood. "I hitchhiked." She needed to stop talking. She was only making things worse.

"Hitchhiked!" Susie brought her fingers to her mouth as she gasped. "By yourself?"

"Only once. It was safe. A trucker. He was a very nice guy." Maryanne forced herself to take a breath. She had to stop lying. "If you let me stay here, however long, you won't regret it. I'll help clean. After work. Or whatever you need." What if they wanted her to do farm work? She could fake an accent, but she had no idea what to do with a horse or a chicken, or how to milk a cow. Did the Zooks even have a cow? She had no idea. Maybe Margaret could show her. Or maybe she could say she grew up on an Amish farm without horses or cows or...

Maryanne was doomed.

Mrs. Zook smiled. "If you can help me with meals, sometimes, that would be lovely. We can work everything else out tomorrow. You must be tired. Where do you work?"

Maryanne gave her the name of the mechanic. "I get a ride with a coworker," she said.

Good. At least that sounded Amish. And it was true to boot.

"Gutt. Very gutt."

Mr. Zook said, "You can stay the night, and we will discuss your plans tomorrow after we return home from our work. There are rules in this house, and I expect you to follow them. No thieving. No men. No drinking. No parties."

"No! I would never—" She might visit Luke, but she wouldn't bring him to their house. And drinking? Sure, sometimes that happened at house parties, but Maryanne hadn't gone to a party of that kind, or any kind, since her parents and brother had died. Drugs and alcohol held no appeal for her. She knew what they did. How they had ruined her aunt.

Joseph said, "Do you understand the rules."

Maryanne nodded. "I promise. I will follow every single one of them. Thank you so much." She hadn't said that the Amish way. "Denki!"

17

Though it wasn't church Sunday, Luke and his family observed the Sabbath by doing only the work on the farm and then resting with prayer and reflection.

Or at least appearing to do so. When Luke closed his eyes, all he could think of was Maryanne. Someone was hunting her. Luke had to do something more to help. He hated that he could not visit Maryanne today because it was their day of rest. And while he knew his thoughts should be focused on Gott, knowing was not enough.

Maybe he could sneak away this afternoon and see her. He had not taken his Kneeling Vows.

Luke sat on his front step, considering this, as

Noah dashed towards him from the field, shouting, "Police!"

Luke's heart pounded. Police? Here? And on a Sunday? Luke's mind flashed to Maryanne, hiding at the old Crawley house. Had they had found her? If so, why would the police be here?

Mamm was in the house, in bed, nursing a cold, and Luke's sister had snuck off an hour ago to visit her friend Esther at a neighboring farm.

Luke closed his Bible and stood. It was a police car. The siren was off, and the car drove slowly down the driveway towards them.

"Should I get Mamm?" Noah whispered.

"Let's see what they want first."

Two uniformed police officers sat in the car, a man and a woman. The man was stocky, light brown with short-cropped hair. The woman was also broad shouldered with wheat brown hair pulled back in a bun. Luke recognized neither officer. The passenger side door opened, and the woman stepped out.

"Excuse me, young man."

Luke cocked his head at the 'young man' as the policewoman was barely older than Luke's oldest sister. "Yes, ma'am."

"Lisa Martinez," the woman said. Holstered at

her side was a pistol. "And my partner, Officer Albert Douglas."

Luke said, "My mamm is coming out. What happened? Is anything wrong?" If there is a fire, he would have seen smoke, and someone from the community would have run to them to help with a firefighting effort at least.

Officer Martinez said, "We found some signs of disturbance at Mr. Crawley's residence, and we believe someone might be squatting there. My partner and I are visiting neighboring residences to see if you or anyone here noticed anything unusual."

Noah shouted, "The house is haunted!"

"Quiet!" Luke said. "I told you it's not haunted."

"You said you did not see the ghost. That doesn't mean it's not haunted. It just means that the ghost didn't show herself. Sammy told me."

Luke made a show of rolling his eyes. "My brother has quite an imagination."

Noah shook his head. "I saw what I saw."

"And what did you see, young man?"

"Salome Beiler. Beanpole killed her and buried her under the big oak. But she's still there. Haunting the house. I saw her at the top of the stairs with a stick. She almost got me. She would have climbed into me and sucked my soul out and taken over my body, that's what Sammy said, and I believe him. Sammy knows stuff."

Luke said, "As I told my brother, I went to the house, and I didn't see a ghost of any kind." That, technically, was not a lie. He added, "Salome Beiler passed on a long time ago."

Officer Douglas cut in. "This Beanpole. I assume he is in prison?"

Luke shook his head. "He was for a while, in psychiatric care, but he's back now. It's been almost two months." Luke seized on the Beanpole angle. "What did you find at the old Crawley house? Beanpole had stored a lot of stuff at the house. Before. They said he had psychological problems. I don't know what kind, but Beanpole had been making a house for Salome. You can talk to Susie Zook all about it. She was Salome's best friend, and she's the one that found out what Beanpole did."

Officer Douglas nodded. He was older, with silver at his temples.

"The elders say Beanpole has repented, and English doctors say he is better. So…" Luke realized as he spoke that singling Beanpole out might send him back to the psychiatric institution. And if Beanpole had done nothing, then Luke's turning police attention back to Beanpole was wrong.

The officer nodded. "This is troubling," he said.

Luke's stomach plummeted. He knew for certain Beanpole was not responsible for the things in the old Crawley house. Luke had brought a lot of things for Maryanne. And the rest, Maryanne had likely stolen. Luke wanted to protect Maryanne, but he didn't want to get Beanpole in trouble.

On the other hand, Beanpole had killed Salome Beiler. And the police would find nothing at his house anyway, so as long as Beanpole had committed no other crimes, he would be fine. Searching his house might vindicate him some in the eyes of others in the community. Though the elders had accepted Beanpole's repentance, others in the community were wary. So Luke could be seen as doing Beanpole a favor. The police would check his home, see nothing wrong, and clear Beanpole of all suspicions. In the meantime, it would give Maryanne more time to get away. And then the whole thing would blow over.

A part of Luke knew he was only making weak justification to himself, but he could not listen to that part. He cared too much for Maryanne.

The front door to the house opened and Luke's

mamm, in a house robe, hastily donned prayer kapp, and heavy beige slippers, stepped out onto the porch. In her right hand, she clutched a handkerchief. Her gaze darted from Luke to the police officers. "What's going on? There isn't any trouble, is there?"

"Just a squatter at the Crawley residence, ma'am," Officer Martinez said.

Luke's mamm sneezed. "Sorry," she said after catching her breath. "We don't have much to do with Englishers."

"Luke thinks Beanpole was hiding things at the old Crawley house," Noah cut in. "But I didn't see Beanpole. I saw Salome Beiler's ghost. Maybe she was trying to warn us?"

"There's no such thing as ghosts, Noah," Luke's mamm said. "But you should look at Andrew Miller. Beanpole. And his mother. Emma was also seen at an institution for her temper. It has improved but…." She shrugged.

Luke's mamm didn't hold with English therapists. She also wasn't fond of Beanpole Miller, or any of the Millers.

"We will pay a visit to Mr. Miller."

Luke's mom said, "It's not just the Crawley house. Some of my friends have had things stolen.

A dress. Some food. And one of my guest quilts went missing along with some food. At first I thought it was just Luke courting with Sadie—"

"Luke and Sadie broke up," Noah said.

Luke sighed.

"But Luke would have returned it. He's a good boy. Besides, who would picnic this time of year? There's a pillow missing too. I wondered if it might be the vagrant, but it could've been Beanpole—achoo—! Plotting something."

Luke hadn't even realized his mamm knew those things were missing. Or the food.

"Do you have a list of the stolen items?"

"I'll write it out. And I'll give you a list of who else I know was robbed." Luke's mamm agreed.

The officer said, "Thank you, ma'am."

"Please, find out who is responsible. My husband passed when Luke was eleven. So when he is out at work, which is near every day, we don't have a man in the house. Not that Luke would harm a fly, but there's something to having a man in the house."

"I'm here," Noah declared. "If anyone gives us trouble, I'll take 'em! Beat him with Luke's old baseball bat."

"Noah, that is not our way."

"I haven't taken my Kneeling Vows yet," Noah mumbled.

"Noah!"

"Sorry, Mamm."

They made further small talk while Luke's mamm went into the house, took a pad of paper on the counter and wrote out a detailed list in her neat, blocky print. She handed it to the officers.

"Thank you," she said. "As you know, we prefer to handle things our own way, but if Beanpole is still...ill... Then the best thing for all of us is to send him back to the institution. They can help them, and he will cause no more trouble to our community."

"Yes ma'am." The officers said their goodbyes and left.

When the car had turned the corner, back onto the road, Luke sat down on the front steps with the Bible, still closed, beside him.

Noah, leaning on the railing, his hands clasped and out in front of him, said "You think Beanpole snuck into our house when we were out?"

Luke shrugged. "No stranger than if it was a ghost."

Noah bit his bottom lip. "Do you think Salome's

inside of me? Maybe I'm the one who is stealing things."

"No! Absolutely not. You have nothing to do with any of this."

"How can you be sure? Maybe it would be better if you lock the door to my room at night. But if it's a ghost was taking over my body, then maybe she can pick locks or something."

"If you were walking around in a dress in the middle of the night, I think I'd have noticed."

"In a dress!"

"Isn't that how you saw her? In a dress?"

"I'm not wearing any dress." Noah clenched his hands together. "I'm not! I'd know."

Luke couldn't help but smile. His brother would think wearing a dress was a step too far.

"Maybe it's not Salome then." Noah stared out into the field. A light rain began to fall, splattering slow, large drops against the hard ground. Noah said, "If it wasn't a ghost, you think it was a real girl? Like, someone living there?"

Luke's guts went cold. "I'd have seen her," he said. It wasn't a lie. He would have seen her and he had.

Thankfully, Noah nodded. "Yeah, you're probably right. Maybe the whole thing was just a trick of my imagination. Sammy doesn't know every-thing. Or maybe it was a ghost, but she's only there because Beanpole was stealing and she wanted to warn us. We don't know."

Luke nodded and put the Bible back on his lap. He opened it to a random section, but he was too caught in his own thoughts to read the words.

Now that the initial shock had passed, Luke realized Maryanne must have gotten away. Other-wise the police would have mentioned finding her.

Maryanne had left.

Luke bowed his head. His throat was thick, his tongue dry, and his eyes stung.

Luke would not cry. He was almost a man, and he had no reason to cry. He and Maryanne couldn't have a future together. She was English. At least she'd found somewhere safe to hide again.

That was all he could ask or expect.

"Maybe I should pray too," Noah said. "Are you praying for Salome Beiler?"

"I should." Not for Salome Beiler. She was in Gott's arms now. But Maryanne, he would pray for her. Pray that she could move to her next place safely, and pray that one day, he might see her again.

18

Salome's voice had faded in Beanpole's third week in the hospital. Or at least he guessed it was his third week. Time ran together there, a string of new drugs and new doctors asking Beanpole to share his thoughts, to open himself up, and to admit his own mistakes.

The last was the easiest. Beanpole's life and been one mistake piled atop the next, and nothing he'd done had fixed them. His birth was a mistake. His childhood, a mistake. His love for Salome a mistake, and his effort to save her life his biggest mistake.

He should have confessed to the elders the morning he woke, clutching her cold body in his arms, her blood soaking into the fabric of his shirt and trousers.

But to admit her death was to turn his back on her voice. No matter if Salome's voice came from Beanpole's own brokenness and imagination, it was all he had anymore.

So he had cared for her. He'd buried her and given her red ribbons on her birthday.

In the hospital, she had been silent. A part of him had hoped, returning home, her voice would come back. He did what the doctors said, took everything they handed him, and told them everything they wanted to hear so he could come home.

But home was silent. His father, Jumbo Miller, never let Beanpole out of his sight. They locked the doors and windows at night, and Jumbo slept on a cot in the hall at the base of the stairs. Beanpole could not sneak past him.

Andrew woke up at the slightest noise.

Maybe Beanpole would have been better off to stay in the hospital. There, he'd had hope. Now he only hoped that if he died, he could join Salome. Not that he expected to earn the grace to join her. He could only wait. Pray for forgiveness. Pray to wait for Gott to take him.

Beanpole and his father had just returned home

from the work site when the police came again. Two officers, one Beanpole recognized as Detective Hernandez, who had handled Salome's case.

Beanpole's hands shook. Had he done something? He could not trust his memory. He could not trust himself. He was a mistake made of mistakes.

Beanpole went back through his memories, searching for gaps. Moments that seemed indistinct. But all of them did. Even now, standing on his porch, the chill April breeze whispering damp on his skin, he felt as though a layer of cotton separated him from the world. Why was he shaking? If they took them back to the hospital, what did it matter? Except, if he had done something else. Something worse. He repented, and he wanted to live a good life. Not a happy one, he had sinned too much for happiness, but a righteous life. One where he could protect the ones he loved, even if he was not a man capable of being loved. Even if he was only a burden.

Detective Hernandez waved at Beanpole. "Mr. Andrew Miller. Beanpole." There's the detective's smile, but there was no warmth in his gaze. It was a show. Beanpole understood putting on a show. He had done it himself long enough. Beanpole formed his lips into a similar gesture. Step-by-step. Pull the muscles of his cheeks, up, up, show a hint of teeth, that was it.

Detective Hernandez had put on some weight and lost hair at his temples since their last meeting. Beanpole assumed he looked older too. He hardly recognized himself in the mirror. His features were the same, but there was a deadness behind his eyes. A slackness to his features. The same comfortable distance between himself and the glass. Beanpole said, "Yes," in the English style.

"Is your mom and dad home?"

Beanpole nodded. Speaking, like expressions, were difficult. He could not hear Salome's voice, and he hated to fill the silence with his own voice. It felt like sacrilege. Perhaps that's why Susie's little girl, Margaret, had felt compelled to speak. He liked her. Her thoughts were clear, like wind through a series of chimes, each note pure.

She's too young to know his sins, and thus uninterested in judging him. Beyond his interest in chickens. Or hens.

Detective Hernandez said, "Might be best if you call him over. Your dad."

But before Beanpole could move, the front door to the house opened and his father, blotting damp hands on the thighs of his trousers, stepped outside.

"Detective Hernandez," he said with a wide smile. Beanpole saw the fear in it. Jumbo glanced over at Beanpole and then back at Detective Hernandez. "I hope there isn't any trouble," he said with a forced laugh.

"Some of your neighbors have complained of thefts," Detective Hernandez said. "Small items. We are checking with everyone in the area."

Small items? But why had they had sent a police detective instead of an officer? They thought Beanpole was responsible. He could not blame him. Beanpole had killed someone. Accidentally, yes, but death was final.

Jumbo glanced over at Beanpole, and his daed's gaze was a blow to the gut. It was one thing for the police to suspect Beanpole. They had every reason to. But his daed knew Beanpole had followed the rules. He had taken the medication, done the therapy, repented, and his own father still suspected him of committing a new crime.

Beanpole said, "I didn't steal anything."

Jumbo nodded. "Can you show me a list of the missing items?"

"Certainly." Detective Hernandez said. "Officer Martinez. Can you read through the list?"

The woman, looking to be in her mid-20s with

light brown skin and hair pulled back in a tight bun, read through the list. "One dress, size ten, one small cooking pot..."

After a few more lines, Beanpole said, "It wasn't me."

Detective Hernandez smiled, and said, "You won't mind if we look around, then?"

Jumbo said, "Don't you need a warrant for that sort of thing?"

Detective Hernandez's smile widened, and his eyes narrowed, the look of the dog who had caught scent of prey. "We can come back with a warrant, no problem. But it makes your son a more likely suspect, considering his history."

"Daed, just let him look."

"Are you sure son?"

Beanpole swallowed. His father's solicitude was worse than any beating. Beanpole said, "Let them look around. They'll see I had nothing to do with this, and they can go find the real thief."

Detective Hernandez asked, "Has anything been stolen from here?"

Beanpole shook his head.

His dad said, "I'll talk with Emma. She's mentioned nothing. But sometimes... She gets distracted."

"Is your wife home?"

"In the kitchen, I suspect."

Emma wouldn't have come out, not with police outside. Beanpole only hoped she hadn't had another of her panic attacks. The medication helped keep her anger in check, but that anger had concealed fear that sometimes revealed itself in staring spells where she would go stiff and still, trembling, eyes fixed on some faraway point.

Beanpole said, "I'll talk with her."

"Best you don't go in by yourself," Detective Hernandez said. "I'll send in Martinez with you."

"Ne!" Jumbo said. "Beanpole, you stay out here. Detective Hernandez and I can go inside. The detective is in plainclothes, and Emma will have an easier time with that. Is that acceptable, Detective?"

Detective Hernandez nodded. Beanpole stared as the two men climbed the stairs and went into the house.

Fifteen minutes later, Detective Hernandez emerged. In his hands he held a square strip of yellowing fabric and an apron." The detective's smile was gone." Mr. Miller," he said, gaze fixed on Beanpole. "We need you to accompany us to the station."

19

Two Weeks Earlier

*R*ain shushed against the warehouse roof, some leaking in a muffled tap-tap-tap against the concrete floor. Maryanne curled up on the ground of the farthest corner, hugging her too-small winter coat against herself, hat pulled down over her ears. She'd lifted the hat and two packages of twelve-hour hand warmers from the pharmacy. The hand warmers were inside her gloves and boots. Four hours in, they didn't help enough.

She should have stayed on the bus. It was dangerous to sleep on the subways, at night, but if

x

she got a nice bus driver, she would curl up with her head wedged between the side and the back on the far back seat. But she hated sleeping on buses. It was too bright, and when they went over potholes, she woke up.

Maybe she should go back Aunt Tracy's house? Billy should have moved on by now, and maybe the next boyfriend will keep his hands to himself. Or at least stay zonked out on the ratty couch with drugs humming through his veins.

Maryanne's throat thickened. She missed her mom, dad and brother. But she'd snuck off for a modeling shoot instead of joining them for James' birthday party, so she'd lived and they'd died. Better if it had gone the other way. A tear ran down her face. Angrily, she wiped it with the top of her glove. Tears didn't help, and she was already damp enough.

Voices, two men and the sound of heavy boots, thud-thud, muffled by the damp, pulled Maryanne from her thoughts.

Maryanne could make out neither man's features. Both were silhouettes framed in the flickering outside streetlight. They weren't addicts. Dealers maybe. The man on the left was too large and too well dressed. The shine on his dress shoes and the line of his raincoat said money. In his right hand, he held his umbrella like a cane. In his right earlobe, a diamond glinted.

Maryanne held her breath. She was stupid to think she'd have this whole place to herself. But if she just stayed quiet, maybe they'd finish their business and go away.

Keep your head down. Mind your own business. Maryanne lived by that code.

The second man, tall and in a navy ski jacket and jeans, said, "I hope you brought the money, Bobby," His voice was light, with a hint of a whine beneath.

"Eight large. I got it." Bobby tapped at a bulge in his jacket at his chest. "Show me the documents?"

"They're safe."

"The agreement was you handed them over tonight. I brought the money."

"And I will keep them to myself, so long you make your payments." The second man laughed, a high-pitched bark. "Cheer up, Bobby. Your dad's gonna be mayor, so long as no one finds out what he did for you."

Mayor's son. Maryanne tried not to breathe. She wanted nothing to do with this.

"We had a deal," Bobby said.

"And we have a deal. Your secret's safe as long as you keep paying. I'll take another eight grand next month, and we'll go from there."

Bobby breathed in sharply through his teeth. "Tim, please."

"Give me the money and I won't send what I know to the papers. Another eight large and your dear dad makes it through election day. You have my word."

"We had a deal!" Bobby scrubbed his fingers through his hair. "Your word is worthless."

"Please, eight-grand is cheap and you know it. Now, where's the money?"

Bobby reached into his coat and whipped out an envelope. Cursing, he threw it on the ground.

Tim knelt, reaching out for the money, so he didn't see Bobby's second move. But Maryanne did. The gun shone, dull steel in the flickering street-light. Bobby's hands were gloved, black leather. It made his large hands a void.

Bobby held the gun properly with both hands, finger on the trigger. His hands shook. "Tim, give me the papers. Now!"

Tim looked up. He stood calmly. "What you gonna do with that, Bobby, shoot me?"

"I'll do what I have to."

"Cops find me dead here, they'll start looking through my apartment. My computer. My phone. Your dad can't protect you this time. Do you really want two bodies on your conscience?"

"She was an accident."

"You were drunk."

"It was an accident!"

"And you left her. It took Charlotte fifteen minutes to die. If you'd called for help, maybe she'd be alive."

"Shut up."

"Charlotte wanted to be a veterinarian, you know. Loved animals."

"I said shut up!"

Tim moved. He was fast, grabbing at the gun. The two men struggled.

Bang!

Maryanne screamed. Tim dropped.

Gun in hand, Bobby whirled around. "Who's there?"

Maryanne held her breath. Stupid. Stupid. Stupid!

Outside, a siren wailed.

Bobby cursed. He knelt to Tim's side and rifled through his jacket, cursing again. Bobby pulled out a wallet, and shoving that and the gun into his pocket, he ran.

Maryanne hugged herself. She was cold, inside and out. How long until someone came? The siren faded. What if Tim was alive? Maryanne couldn't just let him die. She stood and slowly walked to the fallen man. He was still. Too still.

She knelt at his side and put her fingers to his neck like she'd seen on TV. Was that a pulse? She couldn't tell.

Maryanne took out her phone and dialed for the police.

"Please state the nature of the emergency."

"Tim. His name was—is Tim. He's—"

Tim convulsed. Maryanne swallowed a second scream.

The dispatcher asked for Maryanne's location. Maryanne couldn't think. Where was she? She tried to remember the cross street. Spoke, "I think— He's shot."

"We have dispatched an ambulance to your location. Is your friend bleeding?"

Keep your head down. Mind your own business.

From the phone. "Miss?"

Maryanne hung up. She'd done what she could for Tim. She couldn't be here when the police arrived. What if they thought she'd shot him? Nobody would believe Maryanne over the future mayor's son. Her own aunt hadn't believed her when she'd told her about Billy touching her. She was always in trouble. Shoplifting. Bad grades. Running away. Now this. Maryanne didn't need to get mixed up with cops or blackmail.

Maryanne looked down at Tim again. He was still, a small hole in the front of his navy ski-jacket, bleeding stuffing. Maryanne pulled the hand warmers from her gloves and shoved them into his coat.

Maybe Maryanne should stay? Put pressure on the wound. That's what they did on TV.

"Hey!" Someone shouted from outside. "What are you doing in there?"

Maryanne jumped to her feet. "Help him!" she called out as she ran from the warehouse, tearing past an old, brown man who smelled of cigar smoke. Rain pounded her face, dripping into her eyes. She ran until her chest burned and her coat was soaked through. Then she walked and walked, shivering as the rain slowed and stopped, and the first hints of a gray dawn seeped through the clouds.

20

The police interviewed Beanpole until well after dark. They asked about his whereabouts the past two weeks. He told them, as best as he could remember. They asked about the stolen items. A dress. A prayer kapp. A quilt.

Detective Hernandez said, "Looks like there was a woman staying at the Crawley residence. I can understand if you wanted to help her. Like you wanted to help Miss Beiler."

Beanpole closed his eyes. Breathed. In and out. He remembered the feel of the pick hoe in his hands. The bark had cut into his palms as he squeezed it and drew back, desperate to get the teen to let Salome go. He remembered the thunk against flesh and skull and how Salome had dropped. The blood. So much blood.

"Mr. Miller. Beanpole!"

"I don't know her. What's her name again?"

"We don't have a name. She may have witnessed a crime. Did she mention anything about a Mr. Timothy Eldridge?"

"I don't know." Beanpole had never met this girl. Or heard of this man.

"We can't help you if you don't tell us what happened."

Beanpole blinked. His gaze was the shutter of a camera lens closing and opening. Light and darkness. Nothing stopped the images behind his eyes.

"May I see the picture again?" he asked, pointing to the photograph.

Detective Hernandez lowered his brows and slid it over.

"I didn't kill her," Beanpole said. He had to make that clear. He had never even seen her. He couldn't have killed her. But what if he was wrong? What if the drugs and his own memories had twisted together into a lie?

Staring at the photograph, he felt Salome's gaze. But Salome was dead. He had killed her.

Blood everywhere.

What if he had killed this girl too?

Beanpole couldn't trust himself. His father didn't trust him; his mother didn't trust him; his therapist had trusted him enough to refer for parole, but what if that referral was a mistake?

At least in the hospital, he could scream and someone would sedate him. And then he would sleep. And listen.

Silence.

"If we find her, and you do not tell us what you know——"

"I don't know anything," Beanpole insisted.

They kept at it, stopping occasionally to hand Beanpole a cup of coffee, or once, a cool sandwich with dry bread, turkey and mayonnaise and a cup of apple juice.

Beanpole asked to use the toilet three times, and they let him with one of them walking him to the facilities and back to the interrogation room. Beanpole's lawyer from his original case, a short balding man hired by the community fund, had told him not to throw away any cups or containers that might contain his fluids for DNA. But Beanpole tossed the coffee cup, when finished, into the offered trashcan. He did the same with his sandwich, or the remains of it. What did it matter? If he had done something to the girl, and forgotten, then he deserved whatever punishment they meted out for him. He deserved it for what happened to Salome.

What evil was in him that kept him doing horrible things? No matter what he tried, he failed.

Finally, they let him go.

Detective Hernandez said, "We need you to stay close. Don't leave the state. You're very fortunate that none of the ladies are pressing charges."

Beanpole nodded. "May I use your phone? To call the driver?"

The detective said, "Come with me." He led Beanpole to a desk in the middle of the main room covered with neat stacks of paper and file folders. It was dark now, and quieter than it had been this afternoon when they brought Beanpole in.

"Wait here," Detective Hernandez said.

Beanpole nodded and sat on a bench across from two children.

The smaller of the two, a little girl, clutched a stuffed, yellow starfish. One point was discolored, as though the stuffed toy had rested too long in water. The girl's eyes, large and brown, stared into the distance. Beanpole felt a kinship to her. Scared, clinging to something familiar, hoping it helped and fearing it wouldn't.

The other child, tall and thin with a long, oval face, short, curly hair, and large eyes fringed with long, thick lashes, slouched, arm over the back of the girl's chair. Both were too thin. While the girl seemed scared, the boy was resigned. He hoped the two children would be okay. He hoped what the girl feared, and the boy had resigned himself to did not come to pass.

Beanpole might have prayed for them, if it would make a difference. But where had Gott been when Beanpole had tried to save Salome?

The Bishop said they could not understand how Gott worked in their lives. They only could have faith.

Mamm said it was the devil, given entry through one's own sins, which led one to do evil. Or at least that's what she'd said when he was a child. Now, she said little, directing Beanpole to the Bishop, or Beanpole's daed for such advice.

A few minutes later, Detective Hernandez returned. "I'll drive you home, if you want."

"We have a driver," Beanpole said, and at the detective's prompting, recited the numbers from memory.

Detective Hernandez sat Beanpole in a chair beside his desk and, picking up the phone, began dialing the number given, but then thought better of it. "But it's late. A taxi would be better."

Beanpole nodded, and the detective made the call.

Beanpole returned home after midnight. He pushed the door open as quietly as he could. The front room was dark, except for the dim glow of a gas lantern shining in the hall. Beanpole slipped off his boots. No one had called out to him when he came in the house, so maybe his daed was asleep.

Beanpole crept across the dark living room.

Jumbo sat on his cot at the base of the stairs, his back against the wall, eyes shut.

Beanpole swung his leg over the cot to the second stair, then, knowing his dad's neck and back would hurt from his sleeping position, stopped and whispered, "Daed!"

Jumbo groaned and gave a start. "Who's there?"

"Me."

"They let you out then?"

Did he sound disappointed?

Beanpole nodded. "Ja. They want me to stay in the area."

"I want to believe you, son. And you know, no matter what, I will love you."

Beanpole swallowed. His soul was cracked glass. Another formed, blossoming outwards. "Daed, I didn't—!"

"Maybe you forgot something. Sometimes, you forget things."

Beanpole bowed his head. "The detectives are investigating. If there's anything, we will know. I should go to bed."

Jumbo nodded, rubbing his eye. "Ja. Go to bed, son. We have work in the morning."

As Beanpole ascended the stairs, he heard his father mumble. "I've watched him. Lord but I've watched him."

Beanpole gripped the railing. It was true. His father had watched him. Beanpole could almost hear his father's doubts, wondering when he had fallen asleep. Wondering if Beanpole had snuck out in the night and done something horrible.

Again.

"$\mathcal{M}$ary?"

Maryanne's arms and legs felt like lead, and lifting her eyelids required an impressive force of will.

What time was it? Where was she?

"Mary? You mentioned you had a job, and breakfast is ready, if you would like."

The smell of bacon and eggs caressed Maryanne's senses.

Maryanne was with Mr. and Mrs. Zook, Joseph and Susie. They had agreed to let her stay here, and now, she was proving herself a lazy slug.

Maryanne forced her eyes open. Sunlight came through a window at her left. It was well after dawn. Maryanne yawned and sat up. "Thank you," she mumbled. Her bladder ached. How late had she been up last night, worrying?

Maryanne had prayed, and if there was a God, He had spirited her away from the house she was squatting in and straight into the Zook's arms. Such kind people. She wanted to be helpful. Anything to show she wasn't taking advantage.

"Can I help?" Maryanne asked.

Mrs. Zook laughed, a low sound from her chest. "Why don't you get dressed? I have, if you don't mind, a spare dress from when I was younger, before I had Margaret. It might be longer on you. You can borrow it if you'd like. I have some extra pins to if you want to if you want to do your hair." Susie moved the Bible on the nightstand an inch to the left, as though it was out of place. "It seems you might have lost a few. That happens." Susie smiled.

"Denki," Maryanne said, sitting up. The door to the room swung open, and Margaret ran in, leaning her palms on the edge of the bed to catch her breath. "Mrs. Schrock."

Mrs. Zook started. "Here? Now?"

Margaret nodded.

Maryanne said, "I'm fine. I hope everything's okay."

Susie nodded. "The bathroom is to the left, two

doors down. I left you a dress and pins for your hair. I'll be up, if you need anything, just let me know. Food's on the stove."

With that, Mrs. Zook led Margaret out.

Maryanne looked at the chair next to the nightstand where Mrs. Zook had laid a dress, stockings, and apron, and on the nightstand itself, next to the Bible, a small plastic container which Maryanne assumed held the pins she had mentioned.

Maryanne grabbed the container and dress and, after rifling through her backpack for a toothbrush, hurried down the hall to the bathroom. She brushed her teeth and cat washed in the sink. There was a bathtub but no shower. Still, it was far better than the gas station. Mrs. Zook even had a bar of facial soap which Maryanne used.

Maryanne pinned the dress as best she could, tying it with the apron and, after twisting her hair up in a bun, stabbed some pins into it, and then reinforced the look by tying it in place with her thin, black scrunchy. She put the prayer cap over it and went down the stairs to the kitchen.

Through the doorway, it sounded like three people were talking.

"So, it was Beanpole." That sounded like Mrs. Zook.

Maryanne froze as another Amish woman exclaimed, "I knew it!"

Maryanne didn't want to interrupt Mrs. Zook and whoever her guest was. But it would be rude and suspicious to leave without saying anything.

Maryanne's stomach growled. She looked around for a timepiece. A clock hung on the wall. The hands read 7:15 AM.

What time was she and Luke supposed to be picked up? Maryanne wished she had a way to contact Luke. They could track her by her cell phone. How else had they known Maryanne was here?

Mrs. Zook called out, "Mary! Is that you?"

"I'm sorry," she said.

"Come in. Eat."

The smell of eggs and bacon made Maryanne's mouth water. Her stomach growled again. In the kitchen, Mrs. Zook stood by the stove with another, younger Amish woman. The woman's hair was light brown, pulled up in a tight bun beneath her prayer cap. She had a long face, upturned nose, and a narrow, almost pointed chin.

Mrs. Zook said, "Hannah, this is Mary. She's staying with us for a little while. Mary, this is Hannah Schrock. She's a friend of the family."

Mrs. Schrock's eyes widened. "Susie, you didn't tell me you had company?"

"Mary was a surprise blessing."

Maryanne's cheeks warmed. Surprise yes, but was she a blessing?

Mrs. Zook waved Maryanne towards the stove, on top of which sat two metal pans, one with eggs and the other with a mix of plump sausage and bacon. Susie took a plate off the counter and handed it to Maryanne. "Go ahead. You'll want to fill your plate before Joe comes down. He eats enough for two grown men."

Mrs. Schrock said, "It's a gutt thing the police took Beanpole in, considering..." Her gaze flitted to Maryanne.

Maryanne had questions, but she was an imposter here. The quieter she stayed, the better.

Mrs. Zook said, "It's over now."

"Beanpole stole all of those things? And even from Mrs. Fisher! I don't know how he managed it!"

Mrs. Zook shrugged.

Maryanne spooned eggs onto her plate. Who was Beanpole? And what things?

Mrs. Schrock said, "They found some of the stolen items in the old Crawley house. So he must have been storing them there. Like he did with Salome."

Maryanne clenched the spoon. After taking a breath, she placed it back into the pan. Stolen items. The old house. Maryanne didn't know who owned it, but she knew she had stolen things and put them there, so she could use them. Which meant whoever this Beanpole was, he hadn't done it. Maryanne was to blame.

Maryanne bit her lower lip. She should confess. But if she confessed to stealing, they'd never believe her when she said she hadn't killed Tim. A criminal was a criminal. Maryanne shivered. Maybe she was wrong. Maybe this wasn't about the dress or the pot or the eggs or the bread or any of the other things she had taken.

Maryanne asked, "How do they know… Beanpole, is that her name? Stole those things?"

Mrs. Schrock said, "Not her. Him. Andrew "Beanpole" Miller. He's the one who killed Salome Beiler."

Margaret, sitting at the kitchen table, mumbled through a mouthful of eggs, "Was an accident."

"So they say," the younger Amish woman crossed her arms over her chest and leaned back against the kitchen counter. "So they say."

Mrs. Zook nodded. "Beanpole confessed to the judge he had been trying to save Salome from an attacker, and the autopsy, such as they could perform, was inconclusive. They didn't have enough to make a case, and he was... Unwell."

"They found Mrs. Stolzfus' sister's cross stitch, the one she keeps on her counter, in his room. In the drawer underneath his Bible. He said that he doesn't open it. I mean, the drawer with his Bible. It was enough for the police to question him, now they're holding him. Jumbo, his dad, can't pay the bail on his own, so he's going to the elders. And I spoke with my uncle. They will not have the community give money to get Beanpole out again. Not if he's stealing. That makes him a danger. Who knows what he was planning to do. We only have his word he didn't murder Salome, and Susie—"

"Stop!" Mrs. Zook shouted.

"Mamm?" Margaret, at the kitchen table, wiggled out of her chair. "Mamm?"

"I'm fine, sweetheart." Mrs. Zook said. She smiled, kneeling to her daughter who ran to her side and threw her arms around her waist.

"Sorry," Mrs. Schrock said. "Truly."

"When you have your child, you'll realize our words hurt more than ourselves," Susie said. It was the closest to a harsh tone Maryanne had heard from the woman. Susie stroked her daughter's hair "It's fine. Everything will be fine."

Beanpole had murdered someone. Maybe if he also took the fall for Maryanne's thefts, it wouldn't be such a bad thing. But how was that any different from what Maryanne was afraid of? Maryanne had stolen, but that didn't mean she hadn't seen what she'd seen.

"Are they putting Beanpole in jail?" Maryanne asked.

"Ne, not yet," Mrs. Schrock said. "Soon though, I bet."

"Let's move onto brighter subjects," Mrs. Zook said. "The sky is looking gray. Shall we lend you an umbrella, Mary?"

Luke had always brought one for her when he came to visit. Were Amish people just all this nice? And prepared?

Maryanne nodded. "Denki. Please."

How long could Maryanne stay here? A few days? Maybe a week?

She had sixty-three dollars left over from her last paycheck. If she worked another week, she'd have enough money for a bus ticket.

And then she would have to leave Luke and the

life she was building here behind. Leave Tim's murder unsolved. And who else would Bobby kill, by accident or intent, if she held her silence?

And what about Beanpole? He had already killed someone, but...

One crisis at a time.

Maryanne took her plate of eggs and bacon and walked to the table to sit beside Margaret. The front door opened again, and Mr. Zook came in, clapping his hands together and blowing on them for warmth. "Hannah! Why the early visit? I wanted to check if the fence I repaired yesterday was still holding, and I came back and saw your buggy. Is everything okay?"

"Ja!" Mrs. Schrock averted her gaze. "I was in the area and wanted Susie to hear the news before she went into town or someone else came by to ask. Not like gossip. Just because I care for Susie, and I don't want her to have any shocks. You understand."

It had sounded like gossip to Maryanne. Useful gossip.

"I see," Mr. Zook said.

Mrs. Zook explained, "The police took Beanpole in for questioning yesterday about the thefts."

Joseph stepped back. "It wasn't a vagrant?"

Mrs. Zook shrugged.

Mrs. Schrock said, "I said it was Beanpole. They found some things in his house." She explained it again, ending with, "Beanpole is a menace. I told my uncle he should not have accepted his repentance. He should have moved to Indiana with his aunt. Or anywhere but here. Now, they'll see reason."

Mrs. Zook looked down at her hands. She ran her tongue between her lips and nodded.

Maryanne ate her eggs. They were fluffy and hot, far better than a meal bar from the convenience store.

Mr. Zook said, "If Beanpole stole from his neighbors, then I doubt the elders tolerate him in our community from here on."

Mrs. Zook nodded again.

Mrs. Schrock said, "It must be such a relief for the both of you! Susie hides it well, but Beanpole's presence upset her. And he wore that red ribbon."

Mrs. Zook didn't look relieved. She looked scared. "Beanpole must have been planning something," she said.

"Of course he was planning something! Why else would he have been hiding those things in the

Crawley house? The same house where he buried Salome, beneath the oak tree."

Maryanne shivered. Before she had known someone had buried a body underneath that tree, it had made her feel peaceful. She'd sat under it, once, early in the morning when she figured no one would be around.

Mr. Zook said, "I was certain it was a vagrant. How little I know."

Mrs. Schrock said, "I ought to be going. My husband was away overnight on a job. He does construction work, and they pay him extra to work the night shift. But he will be home soon, and I'd like to have breakfast ready for him. You understand."

"Ja," Mrs. Zook said, looking up with a weak smile. "Thank you for letting me know about Beanpole."

"I know how upset you've been," Mrs. Schrock said. "But don't worry. They'll send him away. This time, for good."

Mrs. Zook saw her friend to the door while Mr. Zook took a plate from the counter and filled it with eggs and bacon.

Maryanne, glancing over at the clock on the wall, said, "I must get to my job, I think."

"Whereabouts are you working again?" Mr. Zook asked.

"Mr. Johnson's Auto Mechanic. I get a ride with a coworker and a friend."

"How long about have you been in these parts? I've never seen you at our Church meeting."

Which if Maryanne were Amish, she would have attended.

"Only been here a short time. It was luck I got this job. I... Left home and came here."

Joseph pressed his lips together. "I hope your parents know you are well."

"They passed on." Maryanne swallowed. "With my brother. An...accident." She couldn't tell them it was a car accident. Amish people didn't drive cars, unless they were on rumspringa. "I lived with my aunt."

"I see."

Maryanne couldn't keep lying like this. She felt awful about it. Mr. Zook had been kind enough to let her stay the night and even given her breakfast. She wiped her palm over her forehead. "I'm not really Amish," she whispered. "But my friend is. Luke."

"Lucas King?"

Was King his last name? Maryanne said, "He lives near here."

"I see."

"I guess you want me out now. Let me get my bag."

"Where will you go?"

Maryanne shrugged.

"I appreciate your honesty." To Maryanne's surprise, Mr. Zook smiled. "Jesus commands us to welcome the stranger. You are in some trouble, it seems. I would not cast you out so harshly.

Maryanne swallowed. Her eyelids stung. She would not cry. Tears solved nothing. "Thank you," she said.

Mrs. Zook walked back in. "What's wrong, Mary?"

"Nothing."

"Mary was just telling me a little about her situation," Mr. Zook said. "And, should she wish to call her aunt and let her know she is well, we have a phone in our barn. Now this job...?"

Maryanne nodded. "It's real. I mean, a real job. I just started last week." She looked at the clock over the sink. What if they had left? She didn't even know what time Jerome picked Luke up. Luke would know by now the cops had been to the

Crawley house. If Mrs. Schrock had come with news about this Beanpole guy, then the rest of it would be known too. "I should go. To work." She smiled at Margaret, who was running a piece of cinnamon swirl bread over her plate. "I'll see you tonight, okay?"

Margaret nodded.

Joseph stood. He downed the rest of his coffee in three long gulps. "I will go with you," he said.

"To my job?"

"No. To escort you to meet your coworker. Where is he picking you up?"

Maryanne forced a smile. "I can show you. But it's no trouble. I can just go on my own."

"You are in my care, and I will see you are safe. Do you understand?"

Maryanne nodded. It was nice for him to care so much about a stranger. Though she would only look like more of a fool wandering around, trying to remember the exact spot Jerome had picked up her and Luke, Maryanne was grateful for his caring. Since her parents' deaths, Maryanne had looked after herself.

Margaret asked something in Pennsylvania Dutch.

Mr. Zook smiled and nodded. "Both me and Greta will escort you to your work."

"You three aren't leaving me behind," Mrs. Zook said with a smile. "It's a beautiful morning for a walk."

If Maryanne found the meeting place again, she hoped the large group didn't scare Luke off. Or maybe things would be better if they scared him off. Or if he wasn't there at all.

22

"*B*eanpole! It's past dawn. Your daed said to let you sleep, but you have to have breakfast."

As she shook him, her fingers dug into his shoulder, and her tone was harsh. Like it had been before.

"Denki, Mamm."

Beanpole sat up. His limbs felt heavy. He rubbed a palm over his right eye.

"Did you take those things?" his mamm asked.

Beanpole opened his mouth to deny it, but what if he was wrong? He said, "I don't think so."

"Either you took them, or you didn't."

"I don't remember taking anything."

"What do you remember?"

Beanpole bowed his head and closed his eyes. "I prayed," he said. "About this. I do not think I would have taken what they said. Why would I?"

"Get out. Your daed's waiting." His mamm let go of his arm and left.

Beanpole got dressed and met his daed downstairs. There, Beanpole ate, took his pills, and together, they walked to where the driver picked up them and the other three members of their Amish work crew. Beanpole prayed that the others had not heard of his questioning at the police station, but as Beanpole and his daed approached the rest of their crew, already gathered, two of the men looked up and froze, clamping their lips shut and averting their gazes.

Beanpole's shoulders slumped. He gripped his lunch pail. His chest tightened, and a cold sweat blossomed on his brow and cheeks.

What was the point of trying?

Jumbo called out to the group, wishing them a good morning as he waved.

The other man waved, but said nothing.

When they joined the group, Jumbo waved a hand towards the sky, "Fine morning, isn't it? The almanac predicted rain, but I think we'll get a lot of work done today, maybe even get that roof finished, before anything comes down."

The sky was bright with only a few thick, fluffy clouds floating across it.

One man, a rangy 30-year-old with large, bony fingers, said, "I wasn't sure you and your son would make it today, Jumbo..."

"Why wouldn't we make it?"

"What with Beanpole's...troubles yesterday with the English."

It was against the Ordnung to gossip, but news got around. Jumbo said, "They only wanted to ask him some questions, and they sent him home when they were finished."

The man, named John, but he went by Knuckles because of his exceedingly large ones, said, "Gutt. I know the foreman doesn't want trouble."

"He won't see any from us," Jumbo said. He clapped Beanpole a bit too hard on the shoulder. "Right, son?"

Beanpole looked up and nodded. He tried to force a smile, but his lips barely twitched. He felt scrubbed raw inside. Maybe it would be best if he just left. It would be best if he never returned.

The driver arrived. He drove a large, pea green

van with three rows of light brown, leather seats, more like one would find in an English school bus then in a modern vehicle. The assistant foreman sat in the front seat beside the driver. As the other three men walked towards the car, one pulling the back seat door aside to slide it open, Mr. Marshall, the assistant foreman, opened the front door. "Jumbo!" He called out, waving Beanpole's father to him.

Beanpole's stomach sank.

Jumbo said, "You get in and sit down." He waved towards the open back door.

Beanpole started towards it while his dad went to speak with Mr. Marshall. Maybe Mr. Marshall's coming, and his asking to speak with Jumbo, had nothing to do with Beanpole.

And maybe, on Sunday, on the way to the church meeting, the horses would take flight and they would sail in the air with the clouds before circling to land, handing out baked goods to the children like an English Christmas story.

The two men whispered to each other and Jumbo's face reddened as he stabbed his finger towards the ground, punctuating some point Beanpole couldn't hear.

Mr. Marshall shook his head.

After more back-and-forth, Jumbo called out, "Beanpole, come here!"

Beanpole climbed out of the van. Behind him, one of the other men mumbled, "Good riddance."

Maybe.

Or maybe Beanpole had misheard, and the condemnation was from his own mind.

He went to his daed.

"We will look to you again, Jumbo, for the next job, after this situation has blown over," Mr. Marshall said.

Jumbo said, "They have not charged my son with any wrongdoing."

Mr. Marshall smiled, and he nodded at Jumbo, a touch of sympathy in his gaze. "I'm sorry, Jumbo, Beanpole. You two work hard. You're quiet, and you don't cause trouble. It's just— You understand—"

Beanpole said, "Daed, if it's me, I'll stay with Mamm. They don't have any issue with you."

"Ne!"

Of course. Jumbo had to stay and keep watch over Beanpole. He was not to be trusted. Beanpole shut his eyes. His daed loved him, but Beanpole was a burden.

Jumbo said, "This will blow over. My son had nothing to do with these thefts."

Mr. Marshall nodded again and said, "We have got to go. When this is over, we'll talk about future jobs, okay?"

Jumbo nodded.

Mr. Marshall got back into the van, the door shut and the van pulled back onto the road.

They watched the van until it crested a hill. Jumbo clenched his fists. "It must have been Knuckles. Or Jim. One of them must have talked to the foreman." Jumbo closed his eyes and shook his head

Beanpole's stomach roiled. He knew how difficult it was for his father to find work. Not because his daed wasn't an excellent carpenter and general contractor, but because he had to bring Beanpole with him for every job. Beanpole, the manslaughterer. And now, Beanpole, the thief.

His father's life would be better without him in it. His mamm's as well.

The main thing that had kept Beanpole from ending his life in the hospital was the fear of never seeing Salome again. If he killed himself, the sin of his action would ensure he never ascended to Gott's court. He had hoped when he returned home, he might hear Salome's voice again, at least in his mind.

But Salome was gone. Beanpole had killed her. Maybe being separated from her for all eternity was the just and right solution. Maybe it was the true price of his sins. He might repent, but he could not live a just life. No matter how hard he tried, he failed.

Somehow those stolen items had found their way to his drawers. A part of Beanpole entertained the notion that someone had planted them. But why would anyone do such a thing?

No. He must have done it himself.

And if he had, what else had he done? Had he done something to that girl in the photograph?

When they arrived back at the house, Jumbo waved Beanpole inside. "Go help your mamm."

Beanpole nodded. His daed said nothing on the walk home, but from his lack of expression, the stiffness of his shoulders, and how he gazed off in the fields, he needed some time to himself.

Beanpole said, "I can find work in town. Grocery stores, they need people to stock the shelves."

"We spoke of this. And now——" Jumbo's voice was low and gravelly. "It's best you stay in sight."

"We need me to work."

Jumbo shrugged. "Go into the house and check on your mamm."

Beanpole walked to the house.

As a child, he and his mamm had been close, or as close as one could be to a sometimes benevolent and sometimes capricious dictator. Beanpole had loved his mamm, and he'd wanted to please her. Sometimes, he had even succeeded. Other times it was only anger and impossible tasks, him scrubbing his hands till he bled, him enduring blows for doing or saying something wrong.

Since Beanpole's return, his mamm had changed. Until this morning, she'd been kind, and when her tempers overtook her, she squeezed an orange ball instead of taking it out on him. Once, she even said she was proud of his progress.

When Beanpole entered the house, it was silent. His mamm was not a quiet person. Before her psychiatric treatment, she had taken out her rage on the surrounding objects. The counters had been chipped, the heavy pots scratched; twice, she had thrown an offending piece of cookware through the kitchen window.

After psychiatric treatment, his mamm controlled her rages, but her movements had grown heavier. She said that sometimes it felt as if her limbs were made of lead. Beanpole understood this. Her feet shuffled when she walked. Sometimes, she would stop and lean against a chair or the railing with a creak or scrape.

"Mamm!" Beanpole called out.

Silence.

Maybe she was asleep? Beanpole glanced to the kitchen, and seeing it empty, went up the stairs to where his parents once shared a bedroom. Did she have a headache? It was odd for Mamm to return to bed after breakfast unless she was ill.

Beanpole opened the door to the bedroom and peeked inside. Sun streamed through the window beside the bed. A glass of water, half empty, sat on the nightstand. Beside the glass were two bottles of her prescription pills.

Mamm kept the pills in the bathroom. Walking closer, Beanpole saw the bottle was unscrewed and tipped on its side.

"Mamm?" A chill passed through Beanpole.

His mamm was organized, almost to a fault. Her stay in a psychiatric institution hadn't changed this. If anything, it made her more deliberate in her actions. She took her medications in the morning, the afternoon at lunch, and the evening at dinner.

She followed a rigid schedule and did not leave bottles of pills lying around.

Beanpole crept to his mother's side. "Mamm?"

Mamm was still. Beanpole put a hand on her shoulder and shook. She let out a small exhalation, but her body was limp.

Beanpole's heart pounded. He looked at the bottle of pills. They were sleeping pills. Dated for the previous Thursday, when she got to the pharmacy, for 30 days, but the bottle was empty.

"Mamm!" he shook her again, harder.

Beanpole rolled her onto her side and, knowing what his mamm must have done—what he had wanted to do—he dashed from the house, out the door, towards the road, towards the Schrocks who had a phone in their barn.

This was all his fault.

Dear Gott, don't let me be too late."

23

---

*L*uke avoided the Crawley house, instead taking the shorter way through the trees to the road to meet Jerome. Maryanne was gone. The police had come, and no one had found her in the house, which meant she had to have run off.

Luke's mouth was dry as he approached the roadside. Maybe she would come to the shop and say goodbye? She knew the name. She could call a taxi. But that would cost money, and he knew how little of that she had.

Maybe Maryanne would meet him here?

But as Luke approached the roadside meeting point, he saw no sign of her.

Luke shifted his bag on his shoulder. He'd

packed two lunches, just in case. He could leave one in the refrigerator at the shop.

As Luke spotted Jerome's car driving up, turning onto the shoulder and slowing to a stop in front of him, Luke felt cold. He was back to being boring, everyday Luke. Except worse, now, because he knew how it felt to be something else. He knew what it was like to matter. Luke didn't want Sadie back. He wanted Maryanne. It wasn't love. It couldn't be, not so soon.

Hadn't his daed fallen in love with his mamm at first sight, visiting their district for a month from Ephrata?

Luke was a fool.

Jerome leaned over towards the passenger door and pulled the inside handle, opening it. "Where's Mary? Is she sick?"

"I don't know," Luke said, taking his spot in the passenger seat.

Jerome glanced at the clock on the dashboard. "We can give her a few minutes. I'm a little early."

Though Luke knew there was no point to it, a small, idiotic hope made him a nod.

"They brought in that guy, Miller, the one who killed one of your young ladies." Jerome said,

"Moms was on call, and she had to pick up some kids. And get them placed."

Luke nodded. Jerome's mom was a social worker. She did community outreach and counseling with the local police department. Usually not on Sundays though.

Jerome said, "He's the one who killed that girl and buried her under a tree, isn't he?"

Luke nodded.

"Is that the house where you met Mary?"

Luke nodded again. "Did they arrest him?"

"Naah. Just questioning. Some things have gone missing in your area?"

"Ja. They think he stole things?"

Jerome shrugged.

"Beanpole couldn't have anything to do with that!" Luke said.

Jerome shrugged. "My mom said he looked like he was in shock."

Luke had to talk with Maryanne. Not that he would ever see her again. But Beanpole didn't deserve to be on the hook for the stuff she stole.

Luke had one distinct memory of Beanpole from his childhood.

When Luke's father died, he had been too busy being strong for his family to let himself mourn.

After the church meeting, Luke had gone on a walk through the fields with a sandwich and a glass of cold tea. He walked and walked as the wind picked up and the sky, already gray, darkened. Thunder rumbled, and lightning had danced to the clouds.

Luke had welcomed it. The static in the air, the rumble of thunder and sheets of rain. He'd screamed and cried, knowing none but Gott could hear.

When Luke returned, water slogged, holding the empty glass to his chest, Beanpole had stood with a wind-mangled umbrella at the edge of the field. Their eyes met. Beanpole had given Luke a small nod and waved his hand towards the farmhouse.

No words. No judgment.

Later, when Susie found Salome's body, Luke wondered about that day. What grief had Beanpole been hiding? What curses he needed to shout the heavens where no one would hear?

Jerome said, his voice rising as he shook Luke on the shoulder and pointed behind them. "I think that's her! Are those her parents?"

Luke unbuckled his seatbelt and pushed open the passenger door. Outside, Mary walked towards them, with Susie Zook, her husband and daughter.

Maryanne waved, her smile tight, and called out, "Luke! Mr. and Mrs. Zook walked me to meet with you so I can go to work. I'm staying with them for the week."

Luke nodded. Excitement bubbled through him as he dashed towards the group. How had Maryanne ended up at the Zooks? Where had she slept? In their home? She looked good. Clean. Well rested. Nervous, yes, but good.

"We were getting worried about you," Luke blurted out. "I thought you— I wasn't sure, when you weren't here—"

Luke looked over at Mr. and Mrs. Zook. "Denki. I meet with Mary and take her to meet with Jerome." Luke waved towards the car where Jerome opened the driver's door and now stood, one hand on the roof of his car as he watched them. He called out, "We don't want to be late!"

"Ja."

Maryanne turned to the Zook's. "I'll be back tonight."

Luke said, "I can walk her to your house. You don't have to come all the way out here. I know you're all very busy."

Mr. Zook pressed his lips together while Mrs. Zook smiled. She looked at her husband. "Joe, I think we can trust Luke and Mary in this."

Joseph gave a curt nod. "What time will Mary be back?"

"We finish up around seven. I know it's late, and we've been grabbing a quick dinner at the fast food place, but if Mary's staying with you then we won't do that. It's about twenty minutes to get here, so I should have her back before eight. Seven-thirty."

Mrs. Zook said, "We'll have leftovers for you on the stove, Mary."

Maryanne said, "You don't have to put yourself out."

"I always make extra. Joseph will appreciate not having to take more leftovers for lunch."

Mr. Zook put a hand on his belly. "I like your leftovers. And your sandwiches. And pretty much anything you put in my pail." He lifted a red, metal lunch pail.

Mary said, "Thank you." She blinked after the words came from her mouth, English style, and rubbed her cheek.

Mrs. Zook said, "It's our pleasure."

What story had Maryanne told them? Luke burned to know, but he couldn't ask here. He couldn't ask in the car either with Jerome listening. Maybe he could find a moment alone with Maryanne at the shop. Or, he would have to wait until their walk home. At least Mr. and Mrs. Zook were allowing them to do that.

How had Maryanne ended up staying with the Zooks? They were good people, and Luke hadn't expected them to harm a stranger, but bringing her into their home? Susie Zook was protective of young women, especially those she thought were in trouble. His mamm had remarked upon that, saying 'Susie's habit of putting her nose in where it didn't belong was both a blessing and an imposition.'

And Mary looked like Salome. Luke remembered Salome from his childhood. Dark hair, dark eyes. She had been the sort to say outrageous things and laugh like all were expected to get the joke, whether or not it was funny. Luke didn't remember what the jokes had been about, but he remembered the groups of teens, girls, huddled together and then an outburst of raucous laughter and pointing, usually at Salome.

So maybe Gott had led Maryanne to Mrs. Zook. Maybe they could help each other. Susie Zook was still sad. Luke figured she always would be.

"Denki," Luke said and he and Maryanne said goodbye one more time before hurrying to the car. Maryanne sat in the back. She held a cloth-wrapped package.

Luke asked, "Did Mrs. Zook make that for you?"

"Ja."

"I have a sandwich for you. But I guess you don't need it."

"I love your sandwiches."

Jerome said, "Would you two get a room already?"

Luke furrowed his brow, confused. "A room? Why?"

In the back, Maryanne started to laugh. She asked, "How's Kayla doing?"

"No fair!"

"I never said I played fair."

Maryanne and Jerome continued to tease each other while Luke stared out the window. He couldn't see her face. How long did she plan to stay? She'd said a week with Mr. and Mrs. Zook. After that?

Or maybe Maryanne would stay longer. There was another volleyball game on Saturday and a Sing on Friday night. Maryanne wouldn't know any of the songs, so she couldn't sing. And maybe she was terrible at it. Sadie had a pretty voice. A light soprano that fluttered like butterfly wings.

Luke suspected Maryanne's voice was deeper. She spoke in lower tones, and more slowly.

But you couldn't tell how a person sang from how they spoke.

"Luke, are you okay?" Maryanne asked.

"I'm glad to see you."

"Me too."

"Nobody's glad to see me, I guess."

Maryanne laughed. "I'm very glad to see you too, Jerome."

"Good. Luke was worried you weren't coming," Jerome said. "Did you two have a falling out?"

"No."

They made the left turn into the auto shop.

Maryanne added, "I just thought I might have to leave. Since the people I was staying with didn't have room for me anymore."

Jerome turned and maneuvered the car to the back of the shop for space. "Wait, your parents? They threw you out just like that? On a Sunday!"

Maryanne said, "It wasn't my parents. Just a misunderstanding. Luckily, Mr. and Mrs. Zook said that I could stay with them, so here I am.

Otherwise, I'd have had to leave the district altogether."

Luke nodded. He said, "That's all I heard, that you... Needed a place to stay, but I didn't know where you were, or I would have—" He sighed. Could he have offered Maryanne a place? Then he would've had to explain who she was and how he knew her. Luke said, "I would have done everything I could to help."

"I know," Maryanne said. "I made you a promise."

"You kept it."

"Why do you two have to get so mysterious all of a sudden?"

"My fault," Maryanne said. "How was your weekend?"

Jerome parked, and they went inside for another day of work. As Luke suspected, it was busy. He didn't have time to sit down until after two in the afternoon, when he, Christine, Jerome and Maryanne managed a quick lunch.

They sat at the table in the corner of the floor, with the radio set to Christine's station. She and Mr. Johnson had a quiet war going on where the radio station was set: Mr. Johnson preferred Motown and Christine like what she called "hair rock." After a year of working there, Luke preferred Christine's station, though he wouldn't take a side in Mr. Johnson's presence.

Christine asked, "What are you two eating today?" She had noticed Luke and Maryanne usually had the same sandwich.

Maryanne said, "Turkey and mustard, I think." She held up a bundle and opened it. Mrs. Zook had used shreds of meat from a recently prepared meal to make a sandwich. Not cold cuts.

Luke, whose meal was two ham and cheese sandwiches, both made with cold cuts, a hard-boiled egg, and some left over apple cobbler, said, "Mary, it looks delicious."

"Your sandwiches were a lifesaver," Maryanne said. "If I had known you were still bringing me one, I would have asked Mrs. Zook not to pack my lunch."

Luke's face warmed.

Jerome muttered, "You two..."

Mary, her eyes wide with what Luke knew had to be pretend innocence, said, "What about us?"

Jerome sighed and leaned back on his chair. He had a meatball sandwich on a long roll under a heavy layer of Parmesan cheese. "Never mind," he said with a sigh. He took a bite of the sandwich.

Maryanne asked, "How's Kayla?"

Jerome swallowed, his eyes still fixed on his sandwich and then said, "Good. She's been busy. She said her sister's coming down with a cold. I'm hoping it's just a cold. I thought we had fun."

Marion asked, "Does she text you first?"

"Yeah, sometimes."

"Then she isn't blowing you off."

Jerome raised both eyebrows. "I thought you Amish didn't use cellphones."

Luke cut in, "We can on our rumspringa."

"Then why didn't you get one, Luke? You were on my phone for an hour when I showed you Angry Birds!"

Luke shrugged. "I don't want to get used to it. English life, I mean."

Jerome said, "You might like English life." He held out his hand and pitching his voice lower, added, "Join us on the dark side, Luke. Together we will rule this world as—"

Christine burst out laughing, and Maryanne joined her.

Luke felt alone.

Christine said, "It's a movie, well, a lot of them. Star Wars. You should see it, just for fun.

Maryanne had seen it, and she texted, and she would return to doing those things when she left.

Yes, Luke was on his rumspringa and had the freedom to try out any aspects of English life he wanted. But he didn't feel free. He didn't want to leave his family or his community. And he feared the temptations. He feared setting a bad example for his brother and sister. He feared not being able to provide for his future wife and children. He feared dying like his father.

Luke tried to be brave, but he feared too many things. He said, "Maybe I will get a phone."

Jerome grinned, "All right! We will go after work. Or, wait… Mary, you need to be back right after work, right? Maybe we can all go tomorrow, if you let the people you're staying with know."

"Maybe," Maryanne said. She didn't sound enthusiastic.

Luke wasn't surprised. Maryanne hadn't told him everything, but she'd said enough. She was scared.

The song ended, and a commentator came back with news on the hour.

"A suspect has been arrested in connection with the death of Mr. Timothy Eldridge…"

Maryanne gave a short gasp through her teeth.

"Mary?"

"Shhh!"

"A fingerprint found at the scene was matched to a Mr. Donovan Charles, currently on probation with a prior conviction for trafficking narcotics. Mr. Charles has been taken into custody, pending charges."

Maryanne's face lost all color.

Luke took her hand.

"Are you okay, Mary?" Christine asked.

"I'm sorry," Maryanne said.

"Did you know that man? Mr. Eldridge."

"She doesn't like violence," Luke said. "And Beanpole Miller may have been involved with some thefts in the district. Considering what happened before, with Beanpole…"

"Oh! Beanpole, he killed that poor girl, didn't he?" Christine leaned over to the radio and changed the station. "I can't believe they let him out, and he's living in your district again! I know you are forgive, forget, and move on people, but it seems dangerous. He didn't… hurt anyone else did he?"

"Ne."

"Well, this happened in Philadelphia, far from

here. I'm just glad they caught the person responsible."

"They can't be sure," Maryanne said.

"That's not for us to worry about." Christine patted her arm. "It's okay. Let's talk about something else, okay?"

Lips pressed together. Maryanne nodded.

Maryanne had seen the murder. That was why she'd run. But if they'd caught the man responsible, shouldn't she be happy? Relieved? She didn't look relieved.

Luke tried to catch her eye so they could talk later, but Maryanne averted her gaze, and a client tapped the bell on the front desk, heralding the end of the moment of quiet.

The shop stayed busy until closing, with a lot of inspections, which Luke found dull, and some detail work he normally enjoyed. Now, he just worried about Maryanne. What had she seen? Did the police have the wrong man? If so, she had to say something.

Maybe they had the right man, and she was just deciding whether to help the police make their case?

Luke was dragging by the time the last customer

left and he finished cleaning up his work area and tools.

Jerome asked, as Luke packed his bag. "You're not showering?"

"Not today," Luke said. "I have to walk Mary to the Zooks, and I don't want her to be late." He also had to talk to Maryanne about what happened. She was scared. He had to make sure she knew she wasn't alone.

Jerome clapped Luke on the shoulder. "Good luck, man."

Luke nodded. He would need it.

24

*A*fter taking Mary to meet up with her coworkers, Susie and Margaret returned to the house, took the buggy into town and did some shopping, and then went to Anna Schrock's house, ostensibly to deliver some sewing needles, but in truth, because she wanted to learn more about what happened with Beanpole.

Had he been arrested?

Susie knew she should be glad, but her own actions weighed on her heart. Beanpole was a menace, but if she committed a sin to see him shunned from their district, she still bore that stain. She still had to stand before Gott at the end of her life and explain what she had done.

As Susie pulled the buggy up to Hannah Schrock's farm, Beanpole dashed out from a gap between the fields. Gasping, he bellowed, "Help!"

"Stay in the buggy," Susie ordered Margaret. She jumped out and yelled "Beanpole! What's wrong?"

What if he had hurt another woman, thinking he was saving her?

Beanpole didn't hear Susie. He dashed to the barn and yanked at the door.

Susie ran to the barn where Beanpole was pulling at the latch. His hands were shaking, and sweaty. He muttered something, maybe a curse.

From the house, Hannah called out, "What's going on? Beanpole! Get away from my barn!"

Susie went to his side, careful to keep some space between them in case Beanpole lashed out. "Beanpole? What's wrong?"

Beanpole muttered, "Hannah Schrock has a phone. I know she has a phone."

"Susie, stay away from him!"

Beanpole said, "My mamm! She's— I need the phone to call the hospital. Oh Gott! What if she's dead?"

Hannah ran down from the porch towards them. "Susie, what is he doing?"

"It's okay." Susie said. She pulled up the latch. "Hannah, Beanpole said Emma is ill." From Beanpole's expression, it had to be serious. "We need to use your phone to call an ambulance."

Hannah nodded, and stood between them, fiddling with the latch. "It's tricky, but— The door swung open, and Beanpole pulled at the side of it, swinging it in a wide arc and then dashing through, "Where is it? The phone?"

Hannah pointed to the opposite wall.

Beanpole ran over and picked it up, dialing for the ambulance. He gave his address to the dispatcher and said, "She took pills. Lots of them. At least twenty-five." Beanpole gave the name of a medication that Susie did not recognize.

"My dad, I called but I don't know if he heard me. He was in the fields." He grabbed the phone, hands shaking as he took in a gulp of air. "I left her. Oh Gott, I left her!"

Susie hesitated and then laid her palm on Beanpole's shoulder.

Beanpole sobbed, dropping to his knees

The phone receiver swung like a pendulum on its coiled line.

Beanpole said, "It's all my fault. It should have been me."

Susie's stomach churned. She wanted to offer comfort, but what if this was a confession? What if his guilt was justified? "What's your fault, Beanpole?" Susie asked in a soft voice.

"I don't remember. But they were in my room, so it must be my fault. And Salome…"

"What about Salome, Beanpole?"

"That Englisher was hurting her. Salome was fighting him, you understand. She kicked him and she bit him, and I thought— And I swung, just to make him go away, but I hit her instead. It's against the Ordnung to raise one's hand in anger, and I did, and Gott punished me. It shouldn't have been her. I was supposed to save her.

"I took her home, not my mother's house, but to the house I had made for us. And laid her on the bed. She was already gone. I couldn't even—"

Susie asked, "Weren't you angry at her?"

"Salome? Never! I loved her." Beanpole sobbed, his shoulders shaking. "Salome won't speak to me anymore. I killed her. And now, her voice is gone."

Susie stared down the broken man on the ground. She had done this. She had made a terrible mistake.

Susie could not doubt Beanpole's abject misery. Whatever his faults, he had tried to help.

If planting those items in Beanpole's room has led Beanpole's mamm to take a drastic and horrible action, then Susie was no better than he was. She was worse. Beanpole had not meant to hurt Salome, but Susie had meant to hurt Beanpole. She had wanted Beanpole to suffer, and witnessing his suffering made her realize how cruel she had been.

Susie said, "I will call a driver. You will need to go to the hospital. You and your daed." She looked up at Hannah. "Will you watch Margaret?"

Hannah took both of Susie's hands and leaned in to whisper in Susie's ear, "You don't have to go with him. The man is dangerous. We both know that. They will shun him for these thefts. He has to know that. Maybe he set this up to—"

Susie pulled her hands away. "That is not what happened."

"You don't know, Susie. You're always so kind, but you don't know."

Susie wasn't kind. The weight of her sins lay on her shoulders. She wanted to confess them all, and she opened her mouth, but she couldn't form the words.

Now was not the time. Susie would confess later. She ignored the sense of relief that came from postponing her confession.

Susie bowed her head. *Dear Gott, forgive me.*

Gott was silent.

25

*W*hen they left work, it was drizzling. Luke grabbed his spare umbrella. It was black and wide enough to cover the pair of them.

Maryanne smiled when she saw it. "You're always prepared."

"You don't think that's boring?"

"I think it's wonderful."

Luke smiled. Maryanne loved his smile. She wished she could enjoy it and this walk, but she couldn't stop thinking about the man who had been arrested for Tim's murder.

The innocent man.

Had Tim been blackmailing him too?

They took the long way, falling into slow steps as

they walked from the back of the shop, past stacks of car parts. The air smelled of motor oil and tire rubber.

Maryanne should accept Donovan Charles' arrest as a gift. With Donovan Charles on the hook for Tim's murder, it meant the detectives would stop looking for Maryanne. She could live her life, maybe get to know Luke better, or maybe continue onto California, though that dream had lost its luster over the past few weeks.

Truthfully, it had lost its luster after the accident. If she hadn't gone to that modeling shoot instead of joining her parents for the birthday party, they might still be alive.

Maryanne recognized her good fortune. She had been given two "get out of jail free" cards. This Beanpole could take the fall for her thefts, and Donovan Charles, already a criminal, could take the fall for Tim's murder.

All she had to do was keep her head down and mind her own business.

But could she look Luke in the eye if her silence made two innocent people suffer for crimes they did not commit? What did that make her?

"Can I show you something, Maryanne?" Luke

looked towards a small, concrete building at the edge of the lot.

Maryanne nodded.

"You're not a car person, but it's something I've been working on…"

"I'd love to see it."

Luke smiled again and took her hand. His shoulders were tense as he led her to the second garage. A padlock hung over the door. Luke handed Maryanne the umbrella, reached into his pocket and pulled out a ring of keys. Slipping one into the lock, he opened it. "Mr. Johnson lets me work on her here. I could just put her in the barn, but it's easier, and the sounds and smells would disturb the horses."

"You said you had a car."

"I've been working on Jane for a year." Luke pulled the door open. "Stay here. I have to find the cord. It's cluttered. Mr. Johnson uses this for storage. He owns the land under the whole strip mall, but he doesn't advertise that. He could retire anytime he wanted, but he says he likes the work."

Maryanne wasn't surprised. Like Luke, Mr. Johnson loved cars. She'd seen him fiddling on various projects while the others dealt with customers. "He's working on some modifications for fuel efficiency, isn't he? Something he wants to patent?"

"Hold on." Luke walked further into the building, letting out a breath as something went thump and then rattled along the floor with a metallic scrape. Another step and then light flooded the room. "You can come in now, but wipe your feet on the mat and watch your step."

Maryanne closed the umbrella, shaking the rain from it outside the door before leaning it against the wall. A large, woven straw mat with the word "Harvest!" lay on the floor in front of the entrance. Maryanne stamped her boots on it. Rain had leaked in through the holes in the fake leather. She wished she could get new ones. She had the money, but between nearly getting caught at her previous residence and making a place at the Zooks, she didn't have time to think about footwear.

The room was cluttered, but an organized clutter, except for the hubcap which had rolled into the middle of the floor. A calendar, two years dated, with "Legends of the Apollo" written across the top of the image of a woman in a glittery blue dress, three other ladies in sleek navy behind her, hung on the wall above where Maryanne had leaned the umbrella. Though dusty, the air was cool and dry, the smell of metal, concrete and motor oils sharper than outside where the smells had mingled with the rain.

Luke called out, "Over here," and waved Mary to the back of the room where he stood next to what Maryanne presumed was Jane, her shape hidden beneath a pea-green canvas tarp.

Luke leaned over the car and pulled the tarp away.

Maryanne's eyes widened at the car, a classic convertible, shining candy-apple red, wheels gleaming beneath chrome hubcaps, the interior light brown leather and shining. "Wow!"

Luke smiled, looking down at the ground. "She still needs work. The back isn't finished yet, and the mirrors aren't the originals."

"Can you drive her?" Maryanne walked to the car, fluttering her fingers over but not touching the perfectly painted front hood. She'd learned a lot about what went wrong with cars the last few weeks, but she'd never driven one. Her parents had owned a mini-van and her aunt a ten-year-old Honda she'd bought at an auction and kept just legal enough to pass inspection.

Even so, it didn't take an expert to see Jane was special. Beautiful. And important to Luke.

Luke said, "I've turned her on a few times. She sounds good."

"You should drive her. While you can." Maryanne reached Luke's side and put her hand on his shoulder.

"Will you go with me?" Luke said. "Not now. But..." he sighed. "I know it's asking a lot, and you have a lot going on, but I just thought... I asked you to share something personal, and I wanted to do the same thing."

Maryanne swallowed. "You're perfect, you know," she said.

Luke laughed. "Me? No way!"

"Where it counts."

"I just want to do the right thing for my family and the people I love."

Was Luke saying he loved her?

No, they hadn't known each other long enough for love. And he barely knew her. Besides, if she did the right thing, she would have to leave him. And if she didn't, she would only prove to herself how little she deserved a man as good as Luke.

Maryanne owed Luke so much. She liked Luke so much. And it wasn't enough.

Luke said, "You won't have to ride with me if

you don't want to. Or I could drive you to the bus station. I know you want to go to California."

"I'll ride with you," Maryanne said. The moment she agreed, she knew she shouldn't have. If she went to the police and told them what she had seen, she would have to tell the rest, how she had hidden in the Crowley house and stolen from Luke's community. They'd kick her out for sure. Luke wouldn't want her to go riding in his car then.

"You will?" Luke looked up, his eyes meeting hers, and Maryanne was lost.

Maryanne nodded again, solidifying her mistake. "I will."

Luke pulled Maryanne close, his warm arms a shield between themselves and the dark, dripping world outside this snug, chilly room. The warmth of his lips was a promise and a betrayal. Maryanne closed her eyes and let it happen.

When they got to Jerome's car, he was waiting, arms crossed in the driver's seat. He rolled down the passenger side window as they approached. "You two get lost?"

Maryanne's face flamed. She and Luke were holding hands, and she was certain her lips were red from his kisses. "I'm sorry," she said.

"It wasn't all your fault."

"I was showing her Apple Jane."

"Your girlfriend?" Jerome laughed. "I hope Mary didn't get too jealous."

"I think she's beautiful," Maryanne said. "It's clear Luke has put a lot of work into her. He's going to take me on a drive."

"He is! Now I'm jealous, and Christine's going to be heartbroken."

"I'll take you too. All of you. But not at the same time."

"And not with Mary. I can't take the sugar between the two of you. That's what my Nana always says about kissing. 'Gimme some sugar.'"

Maryanne laughed. She enjoyed Luke and Jerome's banter. She enjoyed her life here, but if she stayed silent and let the wrong man go to jail for Tim's murder, how could she look Luke in the eye?

Luke deserved better.

Maybe it would be better if Maryanne just left. Luke could take another girl in his car. A nice Amish girl without all of her baggage. Someone who wasn't always needing his help.

"Uh-huh. You're supposed to have Mary back home by eight, aren't you?"

"I am. What time is it?"

"Just get in the car. I'll drive you to her house

this time, if that's okay with you Mary. You can always say you got held up at work. It's not really a lie. I know how you are about lying."

"I don't know the way by car," Maryanne admitted.

Luke said, "I do." He opened the back door for Maryanne, who got in and sat down. Luke sat up front with Jerome. "Now that you have a real girl-friend, you should get a cellphone, Luke. Mary, do you have one?"

Maryanne nodded. "It's not charged though."

"Right, no electricity. You can charge it at the shop."

"I don't mind not having it."

"That's so weird. But I guess you're used to it, being Amish and all."

"What if I told you I wasn't Amish?"

"Sure you're not." Jerome laughed. "Buckle up. If your strict Amish relatives don't let you come to work, Mr. Johnson will kill us."

No, Maryanne had to at least go with Luke once in his car. He asked for so little. After, she could leave.

Even if it broke both of their hearts.

26

*A*rtie Marlton, Susie's driver, pulled up to the emergency room entrance. "Susie, can you stay here with your friend for an hour or so? I have to get my daughter, and then I can swing back for you, if you need me. You have my cell. You can call from the hospital." He looked over at Beanpole. "I'm praying for your mom. God's hand is on her. Just hold yourself together for her sake, you understand?"

Beanpole nodded. Susie wished she could stay in the car and ride with Artie, but she had imposed on him enough. Too much. Besides, she couldn't leave Beanpole until she was sure they were at the right hospital. This was the most likely place the ambulance would have taken his mamm, but not the only one.

"Denki," Susie said to Mr. Marlton. "Truly. Thank you."

"Glad I could help. You take care of yourself, Susie, Beanpole.

When Susie and Beanpole walked into the emergency room, Jumbo sat in the waiting room, hands clasped, eyes shut, an open Bible on his lap. Beanpole ran to his daed's side. Susie followed.

"Daed. How is she?"

Jumbo swallowed. "They have a room for prayer, but I waited here for you, son."

Beanpole's breath caught. "Is Mamm—?"

"We don't know."

Susie stood, feeling like an intruder. She did not belong here. She said, "Jumbo. Beanpole. I should go."

Jumbo said, "Wait." He opened his eyes. "You were with my son?"

"I had stopped to visit with Hannah Schrock when I saw him run to use her phone. My driver brought us here."

"Where's your daughter, Greta?"

"With Hannah. It was rather sudden, and my driver needs to run an errand or two before he returns for me, but I don't wish to intrude." Susie hated the gratitude in Jumbo's face. She did not deserve it.

Jumbo's shoulders stooped. Deep frown lines blossomed from his lips, giving him a haggard appearance. His eyes were smudged beneath in black, and puffy. His hands, clasped atop the Bible, were large and chapped. He was not yet sixty, but it seemed an extra decade of exhaustion weighed on his eyes and cheeks.

With a sigh, he said, "I will call my driver to take you home. It is the least I can do, considering the service you have done for my son. Our family. I know it was difficult for you."

"Ne!" She couldn't expect the Millers to pay a driver. Not for her. "My driver will be back for me." She wished he was returning sooner. Now.

Susie had no business being here. And if Beanpole's arrest had led Emma to take her life, then Susie was the last person to offer comfort.

At the same time, she owed them comfort. It hurt her to owe Beanpole anything, but she couldn't deny the truth.

Jumbo said, "If—" He swallowed, closing his eyes. "*When* Emma is stabilized, they will allow us to visit her, one at a time, in intensive care. We cannot overtax her." Jumbo said, "She was almost gone when the ambulance came."

Beanpole gripped the fabric of his trousers. "If Mr. Marshall hadn't sent us home— She would have—!"

Susie asked, "Mr. Marshall?"

"He's the assistant foreman. They—" Beanpole sighed. "They don't need our services. That's what he said."

"Best not think of that now, Beanpole." Jumbo said. "They are pumping Emma's stomach, but then it is a matter of seeing how much her organs were damaged. If we had not come home—" His hands, loosely clasped, clenched. "We got her here in time to save her life. That was Gott's work. If we had returned from the site this evening, as she expected—" He sighed.

Beanpole said, "It's all my fault."

Susie said, "Ne! It is not. It is not your fault at all. We don't know what happened."

The police came for me, and she tried to kill herself."

"Maybe it was an accident," Susie suggested.

"Mamm took up to twenty-five sleeping pills."

Susie pressed her lips together. Swallowing

twenty-five sleeping pills was not a mistake or an accident.

"We don't know why she did it," Susie said.

The door separating the waiting room from the ER opened and a nurse in blue scrubs called out, "Miller, Andrew."

Both Andrew and Beanpole leapt to their feet.

Beanpole asked, his voice loud and frantic over the murmur of other waiting room conversations, "Is my mamm okay?"

"Mrs. Miller is stable," the man said. He was tall and stocky with short, light brown hair, a wide nose and a full face. "The doctor wishes to speak with you, and we thought you might want to see her."

Jumbo, walked up beside his son. "Ja, we would like to see her." He glanced back at Susie. "My neighbor, Susie Zook, has also—"

"It's okay. I don't have to come back with you." Susie had done her duty by bringing Beanpole here. She did not wish to further face her sins.

"It's fine," the nurse said. "Come along. Mrs. Miller is in intensive care." He led them through the door into the emergency suite. "She is breathing on a respirator and not yet conscious. We are assessing her organ function. The doctor will be around to speak with you further."

Jumbo asked, "How long until she wakes up?"

"It depends on the patient. Mr. Miller, we will need your signature on some forms for your wife's treatment."

"Ja. Whatever you must do."

"We can only have one visitor in the room at a time. It's hospital policy."

"Daed, go first," Beanpole said. "Mamm will want to see you."

"Emma will want to see you too, Beanpole."

"There is a waiting area for the families of critical patients," the nurse said. "All who are not visiting Mrs. Miller's room are welcome to attend there."

Susie should have taken her leave, but she couldn't leave Beanpole alone until his daed returned from his visit with his wife. Her presence would be a comfort as they did not know she was responsible for their troubles. Not yet.

Jumbo went with the nurse to visit his wife first. Susie sat with Beanpole in the small, overly bright waiting room. Another family was already there, a mother with a toddler at her side and an infant in her arms. An older boy, perhaps six-years-old, sat at her opposite side, clutching a scuffed action figure.

The boy looked up as they entered. He lifted a hand to wave and then dropped it into his lap.

They sat.

Beanpole said, "Denki."

"You don't have to thank me."

"Hannah did not want me to use her phone. You made her listen."

Susie's guts twisted. A wave of nausea passed over her. She wasn't ill. It was guilt, well deserved. She opened her mouth to tell him what she had done and closed it. Not now.

After about fifteen minutes, Jumbo returned with an orderly in scrubs.

The orderly said, "Beanpole Miller."

"Go with her," Jumbo said. "Your mamm is asleep, now. Go in, but stay quiet."

Beanpole nodded.

When Beanpole had left, Jumbo put his face in his hands. Susie said, "It will be..." She wanted to say things would work out for the best, but she didn't know Gott's will.

Dear Gott, please, see them through this. I do not deserve your mercy, but Emma does. Her actions are desperate, but I drove her to them, didn't I?

If Emma Miller died, the blood was on Susie's hands.

She said, "It will be as Gott wills. We must trust in Him."

Jumbo's shoulders shook. He was a large man, but as he folded in on himself, shaking with grief, the weight of his grief shrank him. He said, "I can't do this."

"You can," Susie said. "She needs you."

"Beanpole. I had thought I could keep my eye on him, but I can't. My son stole those things. He says he did not, but he must have. Already, he killed Miss Beiler. He says he didn't intend to, that was an accident. Maybe you can believe him, but how can I after this?"

Susie said, "Maybe he didn't——"

"Kill Salome Beiler? I prayed and prayed that he had not. But he confessed."

"When?"

"After you found her. But I knew something was wrong before. I just didn't want to believe it. And I wanted to believe him when he said it was an accident.

"Beanpole was odd. Always odd. A social worker spoke with him after he broke his arm, said he might need some help, but I thought I could handle things. The others, my kinner, they all left. And they were right to. Our home was no place for a family." Jumbo shook his head. Taking a deep breath, he looked up. In the too-bright fluorescent light, his skin appeared blotchy. "This time, I won't allow him back. It's too much for us."

Susie waited for the expected sense of victory, or even relief. But nothing came. She had wanted Beanpole gone, and now, he would be gone. But nothing about it was right. Beanpole hadn't stolen. Beanpole wasn't a monster. He was tragic. Broken. Remorseful.

What if he had tried to help Salome? What if Salome's death had been an accident, as he said?

"If Beanpole didn't steal those things, if it was a mistake, or something out of his control, would you send him away?"

"I don't know," Jumbo said.

"Don't." Had Susie really said that? She had done all in her power to send Beanpole away, and now she was asking his father to let him stay? How was Susie any different from him? She had made a mistake, born of good intent, which may have led to a woman's death. Susie said, "None of us are perfect. If we were, we would not be on this Earth. And all of us make mistakes. Mistakes that haunt us."

Jumbo said, "There are limits to forgiveness, aren't there?"

"I can only hope not. Otherwise, what is left for us? If he has not repeated his mistakes, then he deserves another chance. We all do."

Jumbo looked over at Susie, his eyes red. "Denki. From you, this means a lot."

"It doesn't," Susie said. She opened her mouth again, but the confession caught in her throat. Jumbo had enough on his shoulders.

It will do no good. Not yet.

And if Emma died? Should she go to the elders then?

Susie bowed her head, but the prayers were wisps of smoke in her mouth. She breathed them, and they burned.

hen Luke returned home, Noah ran out the front door and down the stairs from the porch, shouting, "Did you hear?"

"Hear what?"

"Beanpole's mamm tried to kill herself. They're saying it's because Beanpole stole all those things. There will be a community meeting about it on Thursday night. You think they'll be shunned?"

Luke rubbed his palm on his forehead. Rain dripped on his open umbrella. Noah, paying no heed, fell into step beside Luke, who angled the umbrella to cover his brother.

"What did Beanpole steal?" Maryanne had stolen her dress and the pot in her borrowed kitchen, which Luke was pretty sure had been Mrs.

Fisher's. Luke had given Maryanne the quilt himself, along with a few other things to make her life a little easier.

So what had Beanpole stolen?

Noah said, "Mrs. Stolzfus' sister's cross-stitch off her counter."

"Mrs. Stolzfus let Beanpole walk into her kitchen?"

"He must have snuck in in the middle of the night. If I'd been there, I'd of grabbed up Mrs. Stolzfus' cane and beat him until—"

"Ne, you wouldn't have! That's against the Ordnung."

"I haven't taken my Kneeling Vows yet."

Luke squeezed his eyes shut. Wasn't that the same logic he'd been using himself? He sighed, "You shouldn't hit people."

"You'd say that. You're on your rumspringa and you do nothing. Live a little!"

"I am living." If only Noah knew how much Luke was living. The memory of Maryanne's kiss tingled through him. And he was going to take her on a ride in Apple Jane. Luke said, "Maybe Beanpole didn't steal anything. Maybe it was someone else." For all Beanpole's faults, he'd stolen nothing before.

Noah shook his head. "They found everything in his room."

"How did you hear that?"

"Sammy."

"Sammy doesn't know everything."

"Ja, but he knows some stuff. The cops came and searched Beanpole's room," Noah said. "The elders have called a meeting about it. Mamm's going."

"What are they going to do?"

"Kick Beanpole out, I guess. He already killed a girl, accident or no." Noah grabbed Luke's forearm. "Hurry! Mamm made chicken and dumplings for dinner, and we had to wait for you. I'm hungry."

That was Noah's way of changing the subject. And in Noah's defense, Sammy was often right about things. So long as those things didn't involve ghosts or other English horrors. Noah asked, "So why are you late? Extra business at the shop?"

Luke wanted to tell someone about Maryanne. But his little brother wouldn't keep his mouth shut, so he said, "We had to make a stop on our way home."

"Ooh, was it a girl? Sadie says you're seeing someone new. It's a good thing she hasn't taken her Kneeling Vows yet because, woo! Sadie was harsh!"

"I'm hungry, Noah," Luke said, opening the front door to their house.

Noah said, "You stay broken up with Sadie, okay? She's…" Noah wrinkled his nose.

At least Luke's new girlfriend had been enough to distract Noah from his original line of questioning. When Luke got to the kitchen, his sister set the table. She looked up, "You're late."

"Sorry," Luke said.

"I'll need you to be on time tomorrow, Luke," his mamm said. "We have a meeting."

"You're going to shun Beanpole, aren't you?" Noah cut in. "Because he stole all of those things."

Mamm pressed her lips together. "Who told you about Beanpole?"

"Sammy. Is Luke going? He's practically a grandfather."

"Noah! Luke has not yet taken his Kneeling Vows, and gossip is against the Ordnung. I know you have a lot of faith in your friend Sammy, but he does not know *everything*. We reserve such knowledge for Gott."

"I'm not saying Sammy is Gott, Mamm."

"Thank heaven for small favors. And as to shunning, we must wait until Bishop tells us exactly what happened before we make judgments about any person in our district. As long as you live in my house, you will follow the strictures of the Ordnung, Kneeling Vows or no, do you understand?"

Noah nodded.

"Do you understand?"

"Ja," Noah mumbled.

"Good, now bring in that bread and macaroni salad on the stove. Luke, can you take the dumplings out of the stove and put them on the table?"

28

*M*aryanne sat in the Zook's living room, on the sofa, a quilt wrapped around her shoulders, knees to chest, heels balanced at the edge of the cushion. She couldn't see her breath, which made it warmer than the house she'd been squatting in. Still, it was chilly enough. And dark.

Maryanne was too scared to mess with the gas lantern Mrs. Zook had given her. Instead, she'd navigated the hallway to the stairs in socked feet using Luke's flashlight. The batteries were near dead, emitting a dim, reddish glow, so she'd taken it an inch at a time.

Once settled, she'd turned the flashlight off and

stared into the velvet dark. Luke had given her the police detective's business card, and Maryanne had put it into her bag. She should have thrown it out. Instead, it, like Tim's last breaths, followed her.

Maryanne didn't want to tell the detective what she'd seen. She was scared they wouldn't believe her. She was also scared Bobby and his dad would make her disappear, the same way they had set that other guy up to take the fall for Tim's death.

What about Charlotte, the first girl Bobby had killed?

Odd how in all of her running, she'd barely thought of Charlotte.

Charlotte had wanted to be a veterinarian.

If Bobby had stayed and waited for help after he had hit Charlotte with his car, maybe she would have lived.

Keep your head down. Mind your own business.

What if Maryanne had to testify in court? What if they didn't believe Maryanne? What if they did?

Didn't Charlotte deserve justice?

Maryanne remembered the warmth of Luke's arms. The way he always seemed to know what the right decision was and how to do it in the kindest way. His last girlfriend, Sadie, hadn't understood that. She was too wrapped up in herself.

Was Maryanne any better? Could she be?

Mary shivered. The quilt was thick, but the thought of facing everything, turning her back on Luke and Mr. and Mrs. Zook and the mechanic shop and Mr. Johnson and everything...

Something creaked, and Maryanne heard footsteps, quiet but steady, coming down the stairs. Maryanne turned her head towards the sound. In the dim glow of a glass lantern, a short, feminine form. Maryanne breathed a sigh of relief. Joseph Zook had only been kind, but Maryanne didn't like being alone with strange men. Billy had been friendly at first too.

But Mrs. Zook didn't scare Maryanne. Maybe because she had invited Maryanne to stay in the first place.

"Hello?" Maryanne whispered. She didn't want to scare Mrs. Zook if she came into this room.

"Mary?" Mrs. Zook stopped in the doorframe.

"I'm sorry," Maryanne said. "I couldn't sleep."

Maryanne shifted the quilt around her shoulders and put her feet on the floor.

Mrs. Zook said, "Don't move on my account. I couldn't sleep either. It's nice to have some company." She crossed the room and placed the lantern on the coffee table. Like all the furniture in her home, the table was handmade and oiled to a soft, beautiful shine.

Maryanne asked, as much for want of conversation, "Did your husband make this?"

Mrs. Zook nodded. "I do not deserve him."

"You deserve him, Mrs. Zook!" Maryanne had never met someone so kind as Mrs. Zook, before.

"Susie. It's just Susie."

"Short for Susan?"

"Ne."

Maryanne swallowed. Her mouth was dry, and despite the warmth of the quilt wrapped around her, her face was still chilled. "My name is short for Maryanne."

"That's not an Amish name."

"I told your husband." Maryanne breathed in and out. She had told Mr. Zook. How hard could it be to tell Susie too? "I'm not Amish."

After a long pause, Susie said, "You were squatting in the old Crawley house, weren't you?"

Maryanne wiped the quilt under her eyes again. She was crying. Her nose was clogged. She'd need a napkin for that. She couldn't get snot all over Susie's nice quilt.

"I understand," Susie said. "And you took some

things. A dress. A pot. I suppose Luke found you, maybe while you were walking around—"

"At the house. He helped me. Not with the stealing. But he gave me things. Luke came because his brother thought I was the ghost of the girl who was buried there. I shouldn't have lied to everyone."

"Why did you?"

"I— I ran away. And then I ran away again, and it just kept getting worse. Have you ever felt like you just keep making the same mistake repeatedly?" Maryanne bowed her head. Her eyes stung. No, she would not cry. Not now. "And if you admit what happened, you'll just set yourself up for worse trouble?"

Susie said, "I know."

"You can't. You're too good. And that's good. You should be good."

"I should, shouldn't I?" Susie wore a thick, navy blue robe tied with a length of almost golden rope that looked like it had once held a curtain. Her robe swept over the tops of her feet, revealing the toes of her slippers. She said, "What if I said I asked you to stay here because hiding your sins hid mine too?"

Maryanne gasped. She raised her gaze to look at Susie. Really look at her. "What sins?" What could Susie have done that was the same as letting the wrong man go to jail for a murder?

"That's the thing, isn't it? Our Ordnung, that's the rules we follow in our Amish community, says if we do wrong and break the rules, we should confess our sins. If we are sincere enough, we're given a second chance. Sometimes. Or sometimes we have to face the judgment. We may be cast out, or shunned. And it would be one thing if it was just me. But it's not. Joe and Margaret will suffer too."

"Do they know? What you did?"

"Ne."

"Maybe you should tell them."

"Maybe you should tell someone what you're running from too."

"I saw—" Maryanne swallowed her words. She couldn't mix Susie Zook up even more into her problems. "If I tell you, it will get you in trouble too."

"The girl buried under that tree at the Crawley's, she was my best friend."

"She was?" Maryanne clutched the quilt tighter. "I stole, but I didn't disturb her grave, I swear."

"They moved her body, after I found it."

"Oh. Good."

"You aren't the only one who stole things, Maryanne. You used what you stole for its intended purpose, at least. What I did was much, much worse."

29

Maryanne shrank into her quilt. "Did you kill someone?"

Susie thought of Emma, in the hospital, and said, "I don't know."

"I won't tell anyone." Maryanne sounded scared. "I promise."

Susie shook her head. "You won't have to." Her resolve had strengthened. It was easier to make her confession to a stranger in the dark. "It wasn't by my hand, but my actions may have... Emma's in the hospital now. She tried to take her own life."

"That's not your fault! You didn't know. You didn't want her to kill herself, did you?"

"Emma's son killed Salome. When I first heard

there might be a ghost, I wanted to go there to see Salome again. But it scared me."

"If I'd known they buried someone under that tree, I don't know if I'd have stayed there. But, I think your friend is at peace. The house, it wasn't weird. I mean, there wasn't any electricity or water. I'd only planned to crash there overnight. I was going to, I don't know, hitchhike I guess. I hadn't thought it through. Then, the next morning, these kids came in and they scared me half to death. But the house itself must have wanted me there. The back door wasn't even locked. If she was there, she wasn't angry. That's what I'm trying to say."

"Salome had a hard life. It's against the Ordnung, but her daed drank at nights, and when he did, he was mean. In the morning, he appeared as sober as any Amish man. But Salome bore the marks. She begged me not to tell because she didn't want to leave. So I kept her secrets. And that killed her."

"Her dad killed her?"

"Ne. Beanpole killed her. His name is Andrew Miller, like his father. He said it was an accident, and the courts agreed. He said he was trying to protect her, but I never believed him. When I found the body, he cried and told me what had happened.

But I couldn't believe him. And I couldn't forgive him. All I wanted was for him to disappear. Which he did. For five years. Then they let him out of the facility, and he came back."

"You must have been— That's awful! Why would they let him back here after he killed someone?"

"That's what I said. I knew the elders were wrong. He still wears a red ribbon on his wrist. Just like the ones he hung over Salome's grave. I knew he was a menace, so I stole some things and hid them in his room.

"I thought it was over. They'd send Beanpole away before he hurt anyone else, and everything would be fine. But then Emma took those pills and now—" Susie's throat tightened on a sob. She had been so foolish. To keep Beanpole from killing again, Susie had lied, stolen, and possibly killed Emma Miller. "They don't know if Emma will live or die, and it's my fault. I'm no different from Beanpole. I wanted to protect our community, and I may have taken a life. And if I am cast out, my husband and my daughter are cast out with me, or I must leave them."

Saying the words out loud made it all too real. What would she do without Joe and Margaret? She would not take Joe's daughter from him. Nor could she take them from the community they all loved. "The police, English, do not have enough evidence to charge. Or so they said. So maybe, if I say nothing…" She shook her head. "But if I say nothing, and even if nobody ever finds out, it's still my fault. How can deserve Gott's forgiveness if I hide my sins for my own comfort?"

Maryanne shifted on the sofa, and Susie, whose gaze remained fixed on her hands, was shocked when the other girl reached out and put a hand atop hers.

"I watched a man get shot by the son of a man running for mayor. I was hiding, and I saw it, but I was too scared to say anything. But I will not run anymore, and neither should you. We both made mistakes, but if you've got my back, I've got yours. We're the same. And we both have to make things right. Whatever happens, I'll always be your friend."

Friends forever, Salome had said, her mouth stained with blackberry juice.

Tears ran down Susie's face. Maybe Salome was still with her, at least in this one small way, offering Susie a chance to redeem herself. "Ja," Susie said. "We'll always be friends."

They sat a while longer, hands clasped, staring at the darkness.

Maryanne said, "I have to make a call."

"There's a phone in our barn," Susie said.

"I remember Mr. Zook mentioned one."

"Joe uses it for his work. We can use it, if you'd like."

Maryanne pressed her lips together and nodded. "Ja. Yes. If you don't mind."

"I'll show you the way." Susie had a call to make as well. Her own grief had haunted her too much to move forward, but Tiffany was right. Whether or not Susie was cast out, she needed to talk to someone and get help. And stop keeping secrets from herself and her family. It was the only way she would find the strength to forgive herself."

he following evening, Susie confessed to the Bishop everything she had done. They sat at the Bishop's table. His wife gave Susie a mug of tea. She gripped it, the ceramic too hard on her palms, the steam rising in foggy wisps. She stared at the steam as she spoke.

"This is a serious offense," the Bishop said. "I understand you are distraught about what happened to your friend, but to arrange for Bean-pole to take the blame?"

"I thought he was a danger to us. To Margaret. I know that does not excuse my actions, but…" Susie bowed her head, hands clasped.

The Bishop asked, "Did you hide the rest of the stolen goods at the Crawley's?"

"No, that was a runaway. Her name is Maryanne. I offered her shelter in our home. Maryanne is a lovely young woman. She has made connections with others in our community. She has asked to speak with you and wants to apologize to everyone who she hurt, if you will allow it."

The Bishop nodded.

"I regret what I have done. I have prayed and begged Gott for his guidance. He has led me here. I could not forgive Beanpole for what happened to Salome. I was wrong. I only hope he can one day find the will to forgive me, and that Emma—" Susie took a breath. She had heard nothing of Emma's condition, and considering her own culpability, had not felt comfortable going to Beanpole's home and asking. Perhaps her hesitance was also because of her guilt. But whatever the reason, the pain Susie caused the Millers was also a stain on her heart. She told the bishop this, and of her own sense of failure as a wife." Susie said, "I understand if you cannot accept me here. I only ask that Joe and Margaret not suffer for my mistakes."

When she had finished, the bishop sighed. "I knew you were troubled, and I should have spoken with you. Perhaps some blame for this lies with me as well. Ask the Millers' forgiveness. Beanpole,

Jumbo, and Emma. And if they accept your explanation, then I— What I believe is of no matter." He leaned over the table, hands extended, fingers curled upwards.

Susie closed her eyes. Her lashes were wet with tears. "I would not have forgiven him," she said. "And I would have been wrong."

"We are all wrong, sometimes," the Bishop said. "I will speak with the police. Emma is improved from yesterday. I visited her this afternoon, and she was tired, but awake."

Susie gasped, the relief flowing through her. "Oh, thank Gott!"

"She has some damage to her liver and kidneys, but with care and Gott's help, she will be healed."

Next, Susie confessed to Joe.

Joe held Susie in his arms and said, "Taking this all on yourself, Susie. I am your husband, and I thought we faced our trials together."

"You deserve a son," Susie said.

"I deserve a wife and a family."

Susie shook.

"And I have both. If you will be mine. Not only in word but in spirit. If only you will let me share your burdens."

"But if I'm shunned. You should not have to share that."

"I promised myself to you, Susie. For better or for worse. The only thing that will break our vows is death."

"I don't deserve you, Joseph."

"I love you."

"And if I am cast out?"

"Then we will find a way together as a family."

Emma returned from the hospital two days later.

"So, it was you!" Emma sat, her back propped up on a pile of pillows on her bed. Her voice was soft and furious. "You did this to us."

Susie said. "I was wrong. I can only ask your forgiveness."

"Hasn't my son suffered enough? Haven't we suffered enough?"

Jumbo put a hand on his wife's shoulder. "Emma? Mrs. Zook helped us, at the end."

"Mrs. Zook came into my house bearing false gifts, and then tried to send my son to jail again. I thought he— And I took those pills, believing him to be a monster. A monster of this woman's creation." Emma raised a shaking, accusing hand towards Susie.

Beanpole, seated at the foot of his mamm's bed, said, "Enough."

"Beanpole!"

Beanpole looked up, his gaze meeting Susie's. "I forgive you."

"Andrew?" Jumbo looked between his wife and his son. "Are you sure?"

"Salome would've wanted me to forgive." Beanpole sighed. "And now I know I can trust myself. So in a way, this was a test, and maybe the gift, to know."

Susie went to Beanpole and knelt, taking his free hand. "Are you sure?"

"Ja. I understand. If I were you, I might have felt the same way. Before the doctors, the therapy, and the medication, I was confused. I am better now. Not perfect, but better. I think that's all we can ask of ourselves."

Susie nodded. "Denki, and if you find yourself stuck with Margaret again, and she talks her head off about chickens, I understand."

Beanpole's lips twitched. "She speaks when others are quiet."

Sun peeked through the clouds when Susie and Joe returned to the parking lot to meet with their driver.

"Is that Luke?" Joe asked, pointing at a cherry red convertible that circled the lot and slowed, approaching them. Inside, Luke and Maryanne sat, bundled tight in ski jackets, a scarf winding around Maryanne's face, both sets of hands in gloves.

Maryanne hopped out of the car. "I'm not too late, am I? I thought you would wait for me. Did they forgive you?"

"I think so," Susie said. Glancing at Luke, she asked, "Did you drive her?"

"Ja," Luke said, smiling. "We had to put the top back up for the highway, but Maryanne asked to pull it down again when we got close to home."

"Beanpole forgave me," Susie said.

Maryanne threw her arms around Susie in a tight, English hug. "I'm so glad!"

"Which means you've got the spare room as long as you want it."

"Denki," Maryanne said against Susie's ear. Then, in a whisper added. "I think Luke and I might go visit his cousin in Indiana."

Luke shouted, "Did you two need a ride?"

"Where will we put them?" Maryanne asked,

stepping away from Susie. "You're still working on the backseat."

"Ja." Luke bit his bottom lip, a sigh whistling through his teeth. "I'm usually more on top of things."

"A pretty girl can be a mite distracting," Joe said, taking Susie's hand. "I know that well enough."

"We have a driver coming," Susie said. "Don't worry about us."

"And don't be out too late, Maryanne. You're still under our roof."

Maryanne grinned. "Your house. Your rules. I know."

After the young couple had left, Joe said, "She is still underage. Shall we tell her we've started a formal process to take her in as a foster child?"

"When they get back."

"And to think, it worried you we might not have another child?"

Susie laughed. "She's more of a handful than a baby. And we don't know if she will stay."

"Oh, she'll stay. I know that look in Luke's eye."

"What look?"

Joe pulled on her hand, and Susie met his gaze. He smiled. "This look."

"Joe!"

"Greta's with Hannah. When we get home, we will have our home to ourselves for the afternoon. I want to celebrate."

Susie smiled back. "Ja, some time together would be good. Considering."

Susie and Joe held hands for the entire ride home. The road, at points, was uneven, but their path was true, and their future set. Together. With open hearts.

EPILOGUE

*B*y the time Susie found the courage to visit the Crawley house, spring leaves burst from the branches of the old oak which had served, too long, as her best friend's burial ground. Susie stood, head bowed. Wind chimes pinged discordant in the breeze.

Salome, I wish you were still here. Then I could race you to the faraway rock and complain about your cheating. I wish you knew I had named my daughter Margaret.

I wish you had been happy, and I pray you are happy now.

Susie breathed new flowers, and as the breeze touched her face, rustling through stray strands of hair that burst free of her prayer kapp. The snake of anger coiled in Susie's chest loosened until it was only herself and the memories of her best friend.

Forgive me.

And in the breeze's whisper, an answer.

Ja, friends forever.

The End

Thank you for reading! I hope you loved reading this book as much as I loved writing it! If so, you can **learn more about my other books here**.

If you enjoyed this book, I think you'd enjoy my book of Darkness Megabook.

When a mysterious woman stumbles, bloody and beaten, onto widower Abram Yoder's Lancaster farm, will he find the faith to love again?

Sofia Angelis is a woman without a past. All she knows is that she's being hunted. When she stumbles, bloody and beaten, onto Abram Yoder's Lancaster County farm, she is not only given a chance at safety, but also the possibility of love. Will the ghosts of Sofia's past keep her from seizing a new future?

Abram Yoder is a man trapped in the past. His

wife Rebekah died in childbirth two years back, and even through prayer, he hasn't been able to absolve his grief and allow himself to live. When a mysterious woman comes to his Lancaster farm needing help, will Abram find the faith to love again?

Join Sofia and Abram as they confront the past, embrace the future and with God's help, bridge the gap between their two worlds and maybe even find love.

Here's a little bit from the book:

Though the rain had stopped, a gentle breeze rustled through the forest canopy, dripping large drops onto the damp earth below. Moonlight peeked through breaks in the thick clouds as owls cried, spiders wove their webs, and a woman slept, collapsed on her side against a tree like an abandoned doll. She had run her socks black and bloody. Her blouse was ripped. Blood seeped from a wound on her temple, matting her hair.

Eventually the intermittent fall of water on her face stirred her to wakefulness. She groaned, wiping her eyes with her hand. Her mouth was dry. Her feet and head hurt.

The woman sat up. "Hello!" she shouted, and the dull echo of her own voice frightened her. Maybe she'd been in some sort of camping accident. She tried to summon some memory of the campsite, what friends might be looking for her, but nothing came. She needed help, she knew that. She felt around the ground for her shoes. Where were they?

She wanted to go home, but where was home? She tried to call up memories of her family, and her heart pounded as she realized she had none. She didn't even know her own name. She had to know her name.

It's a run-down room with the windows boarded shut and the only light a bare bulb on the ceiling. In the corner next to the bathroom sits a damp mattress, atop it a dirty sheet. When she is alone, she can hear the rats skittering in the walls.

She is not alone now.

She stands in front of the mattress, a metal tray clutched in her hands. Though she can't see the man's face through the stocking that masks it, his attention lingers a touch too long. In his waistband, he has a gun. If he comes too close, she can hit him with the tray, but even if she knocks him out, how would she get out of the room? Still, it's her only chance.

He drops six cans of beans on the floor. "Here's

your dinner," the man says, his voice a cruel jest. "Don't eat 'em all at once."

Dizziness overcame her. She leaned forward, gripping at the exposed root of one of the surrounding trees, and dry heaved. Was that a memory or a dream? The sky had begun to brighten — false dawn or true, she had no idea. But once the dizziness passed, she knew she had to get moving again. The trees loomed like hulking brutes around her, and the rustling of the leaves whispered that whatever she'd run from was still out there.

She stood, drawing her arms around her chest to ward off the chill, and walked. Sticks and small stones stung through her socks. She walked through the chatter of birds that heralded dawn, and as the sun climbed, the air warmed and the trees thinned. When she reached a narrow road, she stopped, hoping and fearing that someone might be there. It was empty.

She scrambled down the hill to the road on her rear and crossed the thin stream of tar. In the bright sunlight, the lump of terror behind her ribs began to loosen. If she could just find someone with a phone, she might be able to contact the police or a hospital and get help.

The woman scrambled up another hill and down

again. Walking in the heat had brought the dizziness back, and she often had to stop to close her eyes and catch her breath. Her mouth felt dry and filled with cotton. She had a hard time imagining that she had ever been so thirsty or dirty before. Her cream-colored blouse felt smooth and expensive, and her jeans were cut well for her body. Her nails, though dirty, were even and polished in light pink. She didn't seem the sort to allow herself to fall into disarray.

The forest gave way to fields of green corn. Breezes rustled through the rows, carrying the scent of manure. The whisper of the corn soothed the woman, and for a moment she simply stared, captivated by how the sun kissed the fields in golden light. Beyond the fields stood a large, white farmhouse with an enclosed black buggy parked beside it. Odd, the woman thought, the buggy instead of a car. Yet somehow the antiquity of it made her feel safe.

She walked towards the farmhouse. As she got closer, she caught sight of a neglected tangle of plants and flowers. A garden! Ripe tomatoes hung from the vines, making the woman's mouth water. She could devour them whole. The thought of their sweet juice on her tongue brought on another wave of dizziness. She closed her eyes and leaned against the side of the farmhouse.

A dog began to bark. It was a Labrador retriever, which had been asleep next to the stairs and hidden by the overgrowth of tall grass between the garden and the stairs.

"What's that, Johanna?" a man yelled. "We have a guest?" The voice approached her, accompanied by footsteps. "Excuse me, ma'am, are you lost?"

His accent was strange, vaguely German, and the woman asked herself how she could recognize this, how she could know the taste of a raw tomato on her tongue but not remember her own name. "Yes," she answered, opening her eyes and turning towards the voice.

He was tall, dark-haired, with a full brown beard that touched his collarbone. The beard made him look older, but his skin was smooth and his eyes glinted with a blue that rivaled the bright summer sky. He wore simple clothing: solid pants with suspenders, a white shirt, and a black, brimmed hat that he took off and held at his side as he faced her. He smiled with a stiffness that made her wonder about a deeper sadness, but the smile looked good on him, softening the severe cast of his cheekbones and his forehead.

His eyes widened as he looked over her disheveled appearance. "Ma'am," he said, "dear God, you're hurt! What happened?

You can **learn more about Out of Darkness and all of my books here.**

And if you are interested in getting email updates from me, **click here**.

Lastly, if you'd liked this book and have 2-3 minutes to leave a review, I would be incredibly grateful. Reviews are life and death for indie authors like me because they let potential readers know what folks like them think of the book.

And if you find something in the book *yikes* that makes you think this book deserves less than 5-stars, drop me a line at ruth.price@globalgrafx-press.com and I'll fix the problem if I can.

All the best,

Ruth

ABOUT THE AUTHORS

Ruth Price is a Pennsylvania native and devoted mother of four. After her youngest set off for college, she decided it was time to pursue her childhood dream to become a fiction writer. Drawing inspiration from her faith, her husband and love of her life Harold, and deep interest in Amish culture that stemmed from a childhood summer spent with her family on a Lancaster farm, Ruth began to pen the stories that had always jabbered away in her mind. Ruth believes that art at its best channels a higher good, and while she doesn't always reach that ideal, she hopes that her readers are entertained and inspired by her stories.

Sarah Carmichael has always loved telling stories, and when she met Ruth at a local farmer's market and the subject of writing came up, a friendship was born. Ruth and Sarah brainstormed intensively on Ruth's Yule Goat Calamity series, and worked together on The Long Run series and others. Through this collaboration, Sarah has also gained the confidence to start working on books on her own, which she will be publishing in the future. In her writing, Sarah strives to tell an entertaining story that shows the beauty of God through the seemingly small moments of our everyday lives.

You can learn more about their books at familychristianbookstore.net.

Made in the USA
Thornton, CO
08/03/22 19:35:51